STRANGER IN HER OWN SKIN

Short Stories

WILLIAM KHALIPWINA MPINA

Mwanaka Media and Publishing Pvt Ltd,
Chitungwiza Zimbabwe
*
Creativity, Wisdom and Beauty

Publisher: *Mmap*

Mwanaka Media and Publishing Pvt Ltd

24 Svosve Road, Zengeza 1

Chitungwiza Zimbabwe

mwanaka@yahoo.com

mwanaka13@gmail.com

www.africanbookscollective.com/publishers/mwanaka-media-and-publishing

https://facebook.com/MwanakaMediaAndPublishing/

Distributed in and outside N. America by African Books Collective

orders@africanbookscollective.com

www.africanbookscollective.com

ISBN: 978-1-77934-542-4

EAN: 9781779345424

© William K. Mpina 2025

DISCLAIMER

All views expressed in this publication are those of the author and do not necessarily reflect the views of *Mmap*.

Table of Contents

Introduction

There is an unusual secret in the way short stories unfold—how they begin as whispers in the mind, grow into echoes in the heart, settle as truths in the soul, and finally show up in a book. It cannot be understood by simply imagining it, but by reading a number of them. I decided to come up with this collection as a revelation of such a secret, woven from the threads of hope and despair, loss and love, beauty and brokenness. It is a mosaic of what I have seen, heard, and lived over the years. Each story is unique in the sense that it is a glimpse into the human condition, a short-lived yet profound encounter with the raw, unfiltered essence of life.

Growing up in the rural area of Malawi taught me to see life as it is, not as it should be. The simplicity and complexity of those years are etched into these stories. I remember sitting on the veranda on quiet evenings, the air thick with the scent of rain, knowing sleep would be elusive because the roof was leaking. Those moments, though seemingly mundane, were filled with a quiet intensity—a reminder of resilience, of finding light even when the skies poured darkness. I have tried to rewrite stories that have shaped me, the ones that made me laugh, cry, or simply pause to wonder. They are not just fiction; they are mirrors, reflecting the phantasmagoria of emotions that define human existence.

I have created characters who are as flawed and fragile as they are resilient. Some are dreamers who cling to hope when the world seems intent on extinguishing it. Some are the broken-hearted who find comfort in the most unexpected places. Some are the seekers of beauty, who discover it not in perfection, but in the cracks and crevices of life. These characters are not strangers; they are fragments of us, of the people we know, of the lives we have lived or witnessed.

This collection is not meant to provide answers, for life rarely offers such luxuries. Instead, these stories are meant to provoke thought, to stir emotions, and to remind us that we are not alone in our struggles and triumphs.

I have tried to paint vivid pictures, to craft narratives that sweep you into their ebb and flow. These stories are meant to touch you, challenge you, and perhaps even change you. It is my hope that through them, you will make sense of the world, and in doing so, find the threads that bind us all together—our shared joys, sorrows, and the quiet moments in between.

Welcome to *Stranger in Her Own Skin*. I believe this will be a companion in your journey, a light in your darkness, and a reminder that even in the most ordinary moments, there is extraordinary beauty waiting to be discovered.

William Khalipwina Mpina
Blantyre, Malawi

Neighbours

The sun was about to set. Inside the bedroom, darkness had already fallen. Chiyambi was beating his chest. His lips were moving rapidly. It was nothing, but the sudden disappearance of his wife that had shattered his mind. Upon leaving, she had left a cryptic note, explaining that she could not blame anybody for her departure, but she had to live. Not to be followed.

A wave of despair slapped Chiyambi's consciousness and prompted him immediately to summon his neighbours, Choipa, Moto, and Zanga for an urgent meeting. Having been consumed by a rage he couldn't control; he was to tell them all was not well in his house, and probably get the best piece of advice before he travelled home to tell his wife's uncle.

"Welcome, neighbours." He started the meeting. "Just to let you know that my wife, Mayi Mkulu, has left. From the note that is in the bedroom, she is staying in the neighbouring township, Maladi. She says I must not follow her. This is very painful when I thought I was preparing her for good things. I recall that a decade ago, I wanted to end my relationship with her because I saw this coming, but some of you came to me and convinced me that I should consider the future in which she would take over some of my responsibilities. So many years down the line, you can witness the future I have waited for. See the emotional torture I am subjected to. See the desperation I am floating in after spending my money. She has left me wondering why life has to treat me this way? What wrong did I do to deserve this? Was it not love to send her to school? What is love? Neighbours, tell me. What is love? I sent her to school to match a woman of my status. See, she has left before writing her final year exams. She told her friends that the certificate will be a yoke to the relationship she does not value. I have lost my money. It's painful, but I have to survive it, though I wish to kill myself." Chiyambi whispered.

His closest neighbour, Choipa, looked at him. "Very simple matter." He started. "Please do not worry. The world will never blame you for this. If you had denied her the chance of education, her relatives would have labelled you stingy and inconsiderate. See, you have come out clean. You are making good money. You have all the chances ahead of you. Stand strong. Concentrate on your plans. I know she thinks she has done well, but she will regret it. I am talking through experience. Right now, I am crying for the opportunities I lost during my prime years. I cannot reverse the situation I am in. You may not know what I am talking about. It is inside of me. Be happy, my neighbour."

Moto raised his hand. "I really feel sorry for you. I was one of those who used to tell you not to divorce your wife. I recall when you had a break up it was me who stood on the rift without even your permission. I saw your pains. I felt your traumas and nightmares, but I talked to you, and I said, 'Don't leave her!' I talked to Mayi Mkulu. I said, 'you must not leave!' I came back to urge you to take her back as your own. I won, but why did I do that? I was raised in a single-headed family, without a father and nobody told me why. I heard a lot about my father who never came to show himself to me, who never sent any gift. Honestly, he crippled my past. To add salt to the injury, my mother died suddenly. Guess what followed. Nights of cries. Nights of hunger. Nights of desperation.

It was a painful experience. As these things happened, I hated my father and I made up my mind never to meet him in this life. If you had separated with your wife for good, the grass would have suffered just like I did. Experience says when a man leaves his wife, he abandons his children as well. I never wanted your children to hate you as I rightly do now with my father. I never wanted your children to cry for a 'stupid' father. I wanted them to one day say, our father tried, but it was our mother who betrayed him. It was not for Mayi Mkulu per se, that I knelt down before you. It was for the children's sake.

The brighter side now is that by staying long with your wife and encouraging her to go back to school you have done your part. Over the years, you have strengthened the child and father relationship. The children have a choice now, whether to be with you or to follow your wife. You have been very patient. Continue being so. There is a point in life when one reflects and realizes their mistakes. At that point, Mayi Mkulu will understand that you were not insane. One needs not to think about oneself. Stay well and fit." Moto said with a stroke of regret lingering on his face.

Zanga smiled before he spoke. "I am surprised that my colleagues here are congratulating you for staying with an unfaithful woman for too long. These remarks fall short of sanity. It is well she has left while strong. Last time, you broke up with her because there were elements of rudeness and unfaithfulness. These are signs of a failed relationship. I remember when you told me about this, I indicated that I would come back to you, but I did not. The reason was that I had been approached by Moto, not to intervene in your marriage for obvious reasons. He knows my opinions are always sharp. I do not condone foolishness. I would have told you to leave her, not without facts. Your wife is too loose and playful. I once met her with Moto at a certain lodge in town. I talked to Moto and advised him against this. I told him to stop. It appears your wife had whispered something about your impotence. The children in your house are not yours. They belong to Moto. This is for you to prove. I wanted to tell you this, but I kept my mouth shut. It pained me to carry such a heavy burden. Very frustrating was the news that you reconciled with your wife for the sake of the children. Which children? Whose children? Here he is. He can refute if what I am saying is a lie. And if he is shedding tears now, these are not genuine tears. Maybe you noticed that my relationship with him went sour at some point in time. This is the reason." Zanga exclaimed.

Choipa turned to look at Moto in the face. "I feel sorry for you, Moto. Marriage is a system. There are underlying invisible factors that make the system either strong or weak. You could not be one of the factors to make the system weak. You could have respected your neighbour. He was not a fool to tell all of us here about his intentions to separate with his wife. You came in, but with wrong motives. You denied him to eliminate the pain that kept torturing him. You wanted to be close to his wife. You wanted him to raise your kids. That wasn't right." Choipa screamed.

"Sorry, Chiyambi. Sorry, neighbours." Moto said, while shuddering with fear and guilt. "What Zanga has said is true. I know your wife left because of me; I told her you would not discover what we have been doing. But she has left because she feels she's too evil to stay with you. She doesn't deserve the love and the material things

9

that you give her. Consider yourself a clean man, and please forgive us." Moto cried.

Chiyambi sternly looked at his neighbours before him, and with a smile and a bright face he said, "Thank you! Thank you, everybody. You can go back to your houses. I am relieved."

As dawn broke, a sea of faces swarmed around Chiyambi's bedroom, their eyes glued to the windows like morbid spectators. A chill ran down their spines as they embraced the gruesome scene; Chiyambi's lifeless body hanging in silence. The air was heavy with shock and terror as the crowd's whispers turned to screams, and frantic voices cried out for Mayi Mkulu. She was nowhere to be found, and in that chilling moment, a haunting question hung in the air; where was Mayi Mkulu, and what did she know about the circumstances that led to this tragic event?

When Home Hurts

It was raining ants and lice around Chichiri Shopping Mall. The raindrops were not thick. People were trotting short distances without being soaked. Moya got out of his car. Pulling his old jacket tightly around his trembling skeleton, he scuttled to the ATM. His footsteps whispering on interlocking tiles, he was to withdraw money for his new building project in the township of Ndirande around Goliyo area. The project which had attracted attention of the neighbours because of its elegance had been his dream project since his college days. Such a modern house had never been built before in the neighbourhood of Goliyo. Now he was happy he had made it.

Moya's wife was against this idea of building a house at Goliyo. She had wanted to settle and open a farm back at home or around the Fatima area in Nsanje, where she grew up. Her idea was that east or west home is best; villages had to be developed by those who did well in both education and employment.

Moya had ill-feelings about it. Any news concerning home made him sick. He didn't want to see his feet stepping on red soils along that winding path crossing the tea fields into his home area. He had grown up there. The attitude of the people was not changing. On this he was very clear, and he had told his wife he was not interested in any news about home, and the mere thought of visiting home made his skin crawl.

"Home, I won't go back or if I go, I will slap the leaders." He used to tell his wife.

"Moya, you are insane." His wife used to laugh it off.

Recoiling at the very thought of facing his village folks who had devoured their own resources like a plague of locusts, he stood tall, resolute in his decision to sever ties with them forever. His home, he now saw, was nothing more than a viper's nest—swarming with deceitful tongues, toxic whispers, and venomous plots. Disgust churned within him as he remembered the villagers' insidious scheming, their hunger for others' hard-earned wealth driving them to beg for scraps while plotting behind closed doors. They were parasites, he thought, always leeching, draining the last drops of decency from those too foolish to see through their webs of lies.

The recollection of their deceit made his blood boil, like a simmering cauldron of anger. Every crooked deal, every false smile hiding a panga knife in the back, ignited a fire within him – a wildfire consuming the last vestiges of his patience. He couldn't stand to step foot into that rotting pit again. He couldn't, in good conscience, extend his hand to those who crawled and scraped like lice, bedbugs, and mosquitoes—constantly feeding off the toil and sweat of others without a shred of shame.

Even the village heads, he cried, those supposed pillars of authority, had turned into master manipulators. They had perfected the art of the con, their words as slippery as eels, their promises as hollow as empty drums. With begging bowls in hand, they had been luring the unsuspecting into their traps, promising development while secretly plotting to beef their own pockets. The social cash transfer initiative, a lifeline for senior citizens, had become yet another avenue for exploitation. The elders—deserving, humble souls—were sent away, their dignity stripped away as they were forced to wear tattered clothes and sorrowful faces. Meanwhile, the crooks swarmed in, registering those with no right to the aid, padding their pockets with stolen funds. Anyone who dared to rise above the muck—who worked for a better life—was cheated, their aspirations crushed like beetles beneath a heavy boot.

The stench of corruption clung to every corner, a suffocating miasma that poisoned the very air. As much as it pained him to admit, he knew that the village had rotted from the inside out, a festering wound that could never truly heal. He couldn't bring himself to go back. Not to that suffocating swamp of greed and falsehoods. Not to those who had long abandoned any semblance of honour.

Moya was young when he captured the scenes, and nothing was changing. That became the biggest reason to worry and the subject of discussion between his wife and himself. He often asked his wife why the chief could do that. Who was he cheating? Why did the villagers see a cloud of hope in this malfeasance? Was the chief trying to promote a culture of dependency? Didn't he see the potential of using the available resources and people for growth and prosperity? Moya hated the chief and everybody who was supporting it.

Years later, Moya got wind of information that he was badly wanted at home. This was after the rains had fallen, and floods were reported in most of the areas including the Lower Shire. Moya drove to his house and immediately called out his wife's name.

"Jamila," he turned to face his wife, "You see, people at home cannot be understood."

"What has happened this time?" Jamila asked.

"They met my colleagues and told them I have to go home. What for?"

"Maybe they miss you so much. Didn't they elaborate on why they need you badly?"

"No, they didn't. But I know them much better."

"When did you last visit the village, or my village?"

"Shut up your dirty mouth."

His voice shrieked like a tired hinge. That was a month before.

Back at Chichiri Shopping Mall, Moya was standing in a queue towards the ATM when he saw Yamikani, his youngest sister running towards him, and calling out his name.

"Brother, I never expected to meet you. I do not know the direction to your house. But it has been God."

"How do you say this?"

"Father, mother and everybody were washed away by floods. Their bodies have not been found. I am the only one left."

"Stop your lies. Aren't you growing old?"

She looked at him in the face, and broke down. Yamikani couldn't help it, but cried piercingly on the veranda of the shopping mall. Her voice came out as if something was obstructing her throat. She attracted a lot of attention. Only Moya understood what was happening. She waved at her to cool off.

14

Moments later, they walked to Moya's car, as raindrops were falling on their bodies like small stones thrown from the sky as much thicker clouds gathered from the south. He drove away quickly to hide from both the wrath of the rain and the curiosity of onlookers.

It had been a good year, that year. Farmers were happy because of the rain, but less strong houses were shrieking with pain every time a thunderstorm availed. Moya's neighbours had lost their toilets, and to protect their kitchens from falling, they wrapped the walls with black plastic sheets.

Not long after Moya's sister had cooled off; they started off to the village. They arrived in the thick of the rain, a kind of weather for mid-January. All the roads were muddy, and most cars had packed at the trading centre—only people's feet and not shoes— were moving freely. Shoes in his hands, Moya and his sister went straight to where his father's house was. He couldn't recognize the place. No debris, no family cows had survived. Moya broke down.

Thirty-minutes later, before he wiped away the tears, Moya saw his niece who went bonkers a long time ago walking towards him. Her feet carelessly kissing the mud, she was talking to herself before she could stand a few zero centimeters in front of him. Singing a song of sorrow from her bank of memories, she raised her right hand in the air. He would push her, but he saw that her left hand was pacifying a brick on the back. Moya stood still as her mouth started a new song, suggesting that Moya was a beast. He could neither visit the village nor help his family, but rushed to the village upon hearing the news of deaths. She sang for what seemed like eternity.

The song goes; *Moya, Moya iweee/Moya, Moya iweee/Waona mako wafa/Ndiye wati ndipite kumudzi/Moya n'chirombo/ Moya dzipita kwanu/Moya usatilawule.*

Moya turned his face away and started trotting towards the road that passed through the primary school buildings. In the distance, the song echoed. Dogs barked. Wind shook the tree branches, banged the classroom doors; and a few seconds later, rain battered the ground with much intensity. And pitch darkness fell. Upon reaching his car at the trading centre, he drove away.

A week later, when the rain had stopped and the sky was clear, Moya drove back to the village. All the issues he had with the village had been washed away by the wind of sorrow that blew over him. A slap of reason had sobered him up. He couldn't let his anger put him in a situation of hating everybody and everything. He thought he was a fool. Many years of education he had had at a public university was just a waste. There might have been a difference between wisdom and intelligence. He was intelligent to excel in school, but he was not wise to remember what made him be what he had become.

Moya drove past the space where his parents' house was, straight to the chief's compound. He found him discussing pertinent issues with his Advisory Council of five men and two women.

Without waiting for proper salutations, Moya collapsed to the ground, his knees cracking against the earth with a thud. His chest heaved with guilt, his breath coming in short, desperate gasps. Before anyone could react, he opened his mouth, his voice quivering, raw with remorse.

"I am a fool," he confessed, his words pouring out like hot coals, scorching the air. "A heart-rending fool to have abandoned the village that raised me. A fool to have turned my back on the people who needed me. I am guilty, chief. Please... forgive me... and my children."

His eyes, wild with regret, scanned the sea of faces, but instead of the expected judgment, he was met with a mix of sadness and... Something else. Was it a pity? Indifference? It was impossible to tell. He felt exposed, stripped naked under their gazes.

Then, turning toward his sister—her face pale, her eyes wide with confusion and fear—he croaked, "My sister, please forgive me. I've failed you too." The words hung in the air, thick and suffocating, like a shroud draped over the village. A shiver ran down his spine as he saw the villagers' expressions flicker, uncertainty clouding their eyes. It was as if they weren't sure whether to comfort him... or strike him down where he knelt. And when they saw a rivulet of urine trickling down the front of his trousers, soaking into the earth beneath him, they felt that Moya's humiliation was complete. His dignity had crumbled to dust.

Shadow of Betrayal

The Blantyre City Cemetery echoed with the mournful tempo of the funeral procession as Mike trudged alongside a white casket. In the casket lay the lifeless body of his comrade, John, who had been stoned to death. Mike marched with an awkward, halting pace, his mind clouded by strange and disjointed thoughts. He was definitely in a state of shock, and was following the pallbearers who were changing hands like a bicycle chain.

John's workmates knew something was disturbing Mike, for he could not give a constructive explanation. They watched him shake his head, and wipe tears endlessly. Relatives were left in the dark. None was curious to ask immediate questions. Dumbfounded, everybody was!

Many versions about the death were just circulating. It was death that had arrived but painfully. Death that had come so sudden like rain in the dry season. Death that had probed sorrow to John's wife, John's mother and Nabiyeni alike. Rather, it was death that had provoked jokes from both jokers and backbiters. John's mother wished she had not lived old enough to witness such a death that was recorded stupid and willful. Though John supported his church staunchly, no church leaders were available. It was death uncelebrated. Relatives mourned painfully.

Entering the cemetery, John's beautiful pregnant wife was distressed. She was lost of sanity and power. She could barely understand. Her mind was lost in the wilderness of thoughts. How could a man leave his house, his wife and children, look for a street prostitute and invite a rueful death? How could a man in normal senses walk aimlessly at night in a risky city, a place that was full of evil? She could not be convinced to understand the unpleasant stories that had befallen her lovely husband. She had no muscle to think and talk about it rather than cry. Her major worry was how she could raise up all her six children whom they bore year after year. Her late husband had denied her permission to do child spacing. Now she was wondering how she would manage the children alone without a job. Tears continued to flow on her cheeks as she could not accept that the breadwinner was no more. She followed the procession tearfully.

Turning his neck, Mike spotted a shabbily dressed Ntcheu girl, Nabiyeni, walking between the wife of the city counsellor and a police officer, her well-exposed belly confirming that the hideous thing was done on target. Nabiyeni was the centre of attraction. Comparing her to John's wife, Mike did not want to believe his eyes. There was a great rift between them. Such was not supposed to be, a dirty girl stealing love from an honourable woman. She was allowed to attend the funeral by the authorities who had heard her case. She followed the procession hopelessly.

After all the last respects were paid, the village head's voice trembled with gratitude as he thanked all and gave a solemn nod for the people to leave the cemetery, beginning with the women. Slowly, and with heavy hearts, everybody filed out, their footsteps echoing through the silence. As the sun sank below the horizon, spreading a warm orange glow over the dispersing crowd, a sense of sadness washed over the people, each lost in their own thoughts of the departed.

***

Six months before, John and Mike from the city of Blantyre travelled to Ntcheu. They wanted to ply trade in Irish potatoes. They found a girl guide who took them to the remotest part of Ntcheu. There, the two were told, Irish potatoes were sold cheaply. As they moved, John noticed that the Girl Guide had put on a torn blouse that exposed her twin breasts, which were strong, like two fresh apples. Down the waist, she had a holed skirt that told what tenderness meant to the greedy John because she had no underwear and her body was smooth and palatable. Immediately, John felt for the village girl. It seemed he had a liking for shabby girls who wore natural perfume more than his wife who had suitcases and suitcases of cosmetics that she used to beautify herself.

Donning her worn-out shoes and with tangled hair, the girl's name was Nabiyeni. Every time John's gaze met hers, her heart seemed to sink, her shy smile barely reaching her lips. She was a quiet, withdrawn soul, unsure of herself. But John, ever the smooth talker, coaxed her out of her shell with promises that glistened like sugar. His voice, sweet and warm like honey, wrapped around her like a comforting embrace. His words painted a world of possibility, a life far better than the one she had known. Nabiyeni found herself lost in the belief that this was love, the kind that would lead to marriage and happiness.

"I promise you, Nabiyeni," John whispered, his voice soothing. "You'll never have to worry again. I'll take you out of here."

Nabiyeni's heart swelled with pride. She believed in him. She believed in *them*. In her mind, John was the key to her escape—a man who would transform her from a simple village girl to a woman of means. She had never felt so special, so cherished, as she did when he was around. With John by her side, every doubt she once had disappeared. She convinced herself that he was her perfect match, the one who would change her life forever.

But John, influenced by Mike, deceived her. He claimed he was not married, that he was searching for a village girl to marry. He lied, and they shared a fleeting, intimate moment before he and Mike headed for the city, leaving Nabiyeni in a swirl of confusion and longing.

"Don't worry, Nabiyeni," John had said, "you can reach out anytime if you need anything."

In her youth, Nabiyeni's heart had been full of trust and hope. She never questioned his promises, never imagined that they could be empty. She was too naive, too caught up in the dream of a better life. She held onto the belief that John would fulfill everything he had said, that he would be the one to carry her out of poverty, to a life she had only ever dreamed of.

One morning, she rushed to an Airtel Money service provider to borrow a phone and called John. She talked to him and John was very pleased to have talked with her. But before she revealed the watershed of her call, the line got cut. Taking advice from the Airtel Money service provider, Nabiyeni did not bother phoning again. She simply followed a dusty path that led to the bus stage at Ntcheu boma. She was to meet John and indicate to him that she was pregnant. She vowed not to return unless she gave birth.

Nabiyeni arrived at Mabisiketi Industries just minutes past midday. Her heart raced with anticipation. She scanned the area, but John was nowhere to be seen. A wave of disappointment washed over her as she learned that he was out for lunch. Nervously, she paced back and forth, glancing at the sky every few seconds. The scorching heat made her skin sticky, and the air was thick with dust, swirling around her like a blanket. The sky above seemed to be holding its breath—clouds gathered, but the chance of rain felt uncertain. The winds picked up, and with each gust, Nabiyeni's anxiety deepened.

When John finally appeared, he stopped dead in his tracks as his eyes met Nabiyeni's. For a moment, he froze. His usual confident demeanor cracked, and anger flashed across his face, his forehead creasing with irritation. He quickly turned away; his jaw clenched as he hurried back to Mike.

In the small, stuffy office, John and Mike exchanged a tense, silent stare. Neither spoke for what felt like an eternity. They could feel the weight of the situation pressing down on them. The air was thick with unspoken words, and neither knew how to navigate the mess they had created. Both men were married, their lives complicated by the presence of Nabiyeni—who had no idea of the web of lies they had woven. They were trapped.

Finally, they returned to face her. John's voice was tight, strained. "Nabiyeni, we need to talk."

They tried to explain, spinning stories laced with false promises. "You need to go back to Ntcheu. We'll take care of you," Mike said, trying to sound reassuring.

But Nabiyeni wasn't fooled. She listened in silence, her heart heavy, her face unreadable. Her quiet composure made the men uneasy. She was no longer the naive girl they had once manipulated. She saw through their sugar-coated words.

After a long pause, Mike and John exchanged glances. The reality was setting in. They couldn't convince her to go back to Ntcheu—not after everything. "Wait here for a while," John muttered, his voice edged with impatience. "We'll finish up soon, and then we can sort things out."

They instructed her to stay at a distance, as their boss—a notoriously angry woman—wouldn't tolerate anyone loitering near the office gates for too long.

Nabiyeni nodded, though every muscle in her body screamed to do something—anything—to stop them from leaving. But she obeyed, waiting in the scorching heat, feeling more abandoned. Time seemed to stretch endlessly.

Hours later, when the sun hidden in the clouds of rain began its descent, John and Mike slipped quietly through the back door of the office. They hadn't found a way to help her. No money for transport. No solution for accommodation. Just empty promises left to wither in the heat.

Nabiyeni stood there. Her heart sank deeper than the fading sun. She was alone again. Soon, the dark clouds were blanketing the sky and thunder was rumbling fiercely. Having not known that the men had fled, Nabiyeni felt that she had waited enough. She went back to the gateman and found out that all the workers had gone. The offices were closed.

The sun had already sunk, and night was encroaching. Tears welled up in her small eyelids, threatening to spill over. Panic surged within her—she had no money for transport back home. The unfamiliar city loomed large, and she couldn't even remember where John had said his house was. Overcome by a sense of helplessness, she began walking aimlessly, her feet carrying her with no clear destination. Her mind raced with thoughts of finding refuge in Blantyre with distant relatives, but the hope quickly withered—there was no one. She briefly considered asking the police for help, but the idea filled her with dread. The chilling stories of officers exploiting vulnerable girls played like a warning in her mind, and the thought was swiftly smothered. Defeated, she slumped down beneath the faint glow of a security light, its weak beam struggling against the relentless downpour, while others hurriedly sought shelter. The rain soaked through her clothes, its coldness merging with the icy grip of fear that threatened to swallow her. With no other choice, she reluctantly pushed herself to her feet and, heart pounding, ventured into the enveloping darkness of Magalasi Road.

John sat in the chair, his mind spinning in a chaotic whirlwind. It was already 8 p.m., and his confusion deepened. He clenched his fists in frustration, then suddenly shot to his feet. His heart raced as he glanced nervously at the clock. He couldn't stay here any longer. He couldn't ignore the knot of guilt tightening in his chest. Without a word to his wife, he slipped out the door and onto the main road.

The rain had started to pour, hammering the earth like a thousand drum beats. Lightning flashed violently in the distance, its jagged glow lighting up the darkened streets. John's feet splashed through puddles, the cold water soaking through his shoes, but he barely noticed. His mind was elsewhere.

Minutes later, he arrived at Mike's house, his breath coming in sharp gasps. Mike, the mastermind behind their twisted plan, was the one who had convinced him to abandon Nabiyeni. But now, standing in the rain-soaked night, John's conscience screamed at him. He could hardly bear the thought of what they'd done to that innocent girl.

As he knocked on the door, his heart pounded in his chest, a fierce drumbeat of regret. The door creaked open, and Mike's voice, low and cautious, greeted him. "What brings you here at this odd hour?" he whispered, his eyes darting around, checking for anyone who might overhear.

"I... It's about Nabiyeni," John stammered, swallowing hard. His voice was shaky, filled with an undercurrent of fear. "I fear for her safety. You know she's just a village girl. She doesn't know what's out there."

Mike's eyes narrowed, but he didn't answer right away. Instead, he leaned in, his breath warm on John's ear. "What about her?"

But before John could respond, the sound of a car door slamming shut interrupted their conversation. Both men froze. A figure appeared at the doorway—Mike's wife, her presence like a sudden storm crashing into their dark secret. Her eyes flicked from one man to the other, suspicion heavy in her gaze.

In an instant, the atmosphere shifted. The tension between John and Mike evaporated as they both grew silent, aware that their secret was hanging by a thread. Outside, the rain continued to pound against the house with a fury that matched the turmoil inside. The roof groaned, and water began to drip from the ceiling, pooling on the floor as Mike's children gathered near the door, their eyes wide with curiosity. The room, once a place of whispered plans, now felt suffocating and full of tension.

As the rain intensified, the leaks grew worse, and the room grew darker, mirroring the deepening dread in John's heart. Every creak of the roof made his stomach twist. He could hardly breathe. He could already hear the whispers of the city—the rumours about serial killers, about women disappearing in the night. What if it was too late for Nabiyeni? He couldn't shake the image of her alone, vulnerable, lost in the city. The guilt gnawed at him.

Suddenly, he couldn't sit there any longer. He exploded from his seat, his hands shaking with a mix of fury and fear. Without a word, he stormed out of the house, slamming the door behind him. The sound echoed in the night, sharp and final.

John plunged into the rain-soaked street, the cold-water biting at his skin, but it barely registered. His mind was laser-focused on one thing: finding Nabiyeni before it was too late. His breath came in ragged bursts as he disappeared into the darkness, the night swallowing him whole.

Nabiyeni stumbled through the dark streets. Her mind was clouded with fear and uncertainty. The lights from the city buildings flickered dimly, offering little comfort. Her eyes darted around

Magalasi road, and it wasn't long before she noticed a figure behind her, moving quickly in the shadows. Her heart skipped a beat. The haunting stories of serial killers she'd heard in the city replayed in her mind, and grew louder. Panic surged through her veins, and without thinking, she broke into a run, her breath coming in ragged gasps.

The man behind her sprinted even faster, calling out, "Stop! It's me, Nabiyeni! Stop!"

But she couldn't stop. The fear was suffocating, urging her to run faster. Her legs ached, but the adrenaline kept her going. She glanced over her shoulder—he was still gaining on her. Desperation flooded her, and in a blur of instinct, she veered off the street, following the railway line. There, she saw a large stone resting in the dirt.

Her mind raced—was this the end? Was he going to kill her? — and without a second thought, she grabbed the stone with trembling hands. Her palms were slick with sweat, her heart hammering in her chest. She crouched down, clutching it tightly, ready to defend herself. The footsteps grew louder, closer. She held her breath.

Then, just as the man's figure loomed near, Nabiyeni pounced. Like a lion starved for prey, she slammed the stone against his body, knocking him to the ground with a brutal force. Her body shook with terror, but her mind was resolute. She screamed, her voice raw and desperate. "Help! Somebody, please help!"

Within moments, the sound of a G4S patrol vehicle echoed, its sirens cutting through the night. The vehicle screeched to a halt, and four security guards rushed out, their hands quickly grabbing the groaning man from the ground. His face was twisted in pain, but there was something unsettling in his eyes. The guards shoved him into the back of the vehicle, then turned to Nabiyeni. "Get in," one of them commanded. His tone was cold, but urgent.

Nabiyeni climbed into the patrol car, still shaking, her heart barely able to keep up with the speed of her thoughts. The vehicle sped off, back to the city, the lights flashing through the rain-soaked street, and they arrived at Blantyre Police Station in a matter of minutes.

Inside, the atmosphere was tense and clinical. The officers took their statements, but Nabiyeni couldn't focus on the questions. Her hands trembled as she recounted the events, still in shock from what had just happened. When she was asked to identify the man, she could hardly believe her own words. Her eyes locked on the man who lay there, his face bruised and his breath shallow. John? Her mind spun. The man she thought she could trust. The man who had promised her a better life.

She could hardly speak as she looked at him, the realization crashing over her like a wave. "It's him," she whispered, her voice thick with disbelief. "It's John."

A cold silence followed, heavy with the weight of her words. Tears welled up in Nabiyeni's eyes, but they didn't fall. The finality of it all was too much. She had come so far, only to discover that the man she had once believed in was the one who had betrayed her.

"I... I didn't know," she whispered, guilt choking her. "I didn't know..."

But it was too late. John's life was slipping away. The damage had been done. His breath grew weaker, and his eyes glazed over, staring up at the ceiling of the police station. And with that, the man who had shattered her life was gone—his lies, his promises, all lost in the cold grip of death.

Nabiyeni's tears finally fell, but they did nothing to bring him back. She had saved herself, but at what cost? The life she had imagined with John was now a distant, painful memory.

Footsteps

It was cold and windy that night, but it wasn't the cyclone ravaging Mozambique, destroying property and claiming lives. No, it was just the familiar chill of June, the kind that always seems to bite a little harder from Dedza Mountain. Bitter cold winds cut through the broken window. A creeping sense of impending doom—like death itself lingered in the air, masked by an odd, hollow laughter. I couldn't stand it anymore. My wife and I had been quarrelling over something so trivial, yet it felt like the world was disentangling. I had forgotten to buy her a birthday present. She was hurt, though I couldn't understand why she couldn't see that it wasn't intentional. My frustration mounted as I realized I couldn't make her understand, and in my anger, I snapped: if she wouldn't understand, then I wouldn't either. I stormed out of the house, desperate to escape the suffocating tension. I sought refuge in a room at Dedza Mountain View Lodge, far from the echoes of our argument, far from the weight of everything that was happening that time.

Around midnight, I lay awake, my body rigid and frozen, every muscle tense with unease. Only my eyes moved, darting around the room, as my mind raced in silence. The midnight breeze whispered through the window, and I wondered how nature, in its cruel indifference, had conspired to make me feel like a coward. Then, I heard it—footsteps. Soft, deliberate taps on the white tiles of the floor. Footsteps that seemed to haunt me. They sent a ripple of dread through my spine. My head jerked, a shiver of fear running down my neck, and my ears strained, desperate to make sense of the sound.

The footsteps didn't just walk; they danced, almost mockingly, growing louder and nearer to my door. I lay there, paralysed, my thoughts circling. Had I told the receptionist I greeted at the counter to follow me to my room? My stomach churned with unease as I questioned myself. In the adjacent room, a man coughed, breaking the tension, but the footsteps didn't stop. They lingered—footsteps that felt like a shadow, weaving through the building, deliberately drawing closer to me, until they stopped at the very end of the hall, just outside my door. The silence that followed felt suffocating.

Sleep fled from my eyes, slipping away like water through my fingers. There was something unsettling about that night—the coldness that seeped into the building, the wind howling through the cracks, and those footsteps, echoing faintly in the hallway. They lingered, refusing to be dismissed, just like the rain that couldn't seem to stop falling. Waves of worry churned inside me, tightening my chest. I sat up on the bed, my mind racing, trying to make sense of it all. Who owned those footsteps? Why did they follow me? My thoughts spiralled, consumed by suspicion—who had spoken of me? I hadn't done anything to warrant this kind of attention. I began to feel a cold knot of panic settle in my stomach, but then, just as quickly, a thought struck me, and a flicker of relief washed over my face. I didn't owe an explanation to anyone. I didn't need to answer to strangers or face whatever shadow was lurking outside my door. I had the right to enjoy this solitude, this rare moment of freedom. I pulled the thick blanket over my head, as if to shield myself from the restless thoughts and the creeping sense of dread. Closing my eyes, I tried to quieten my mind, telling myself to lie still, to resist the urge to give in to panic.

It would be wise to say, at this point, that I didn't just choose to stay in this room. Not at all. I must repeat that I had fled from my marital home, desperate to escape the suffocating weight of it all. In my frantic search for some semblance of freedom, I found this sterile hotel room, but it was no sanctuary. There was no peace here. None. Maybe, my wife, Anna, knew what was going on. Earlier that day, she deliberately chose not to understand me, ignoring the turmoil I was in. I had told her, honestly, that her attitude disgusted me, but she dismissed my feelings as though they were irrelevant. She chose to ignore my decision, brushing it aside as if it were nothing. And for the simple fact that I had never loved her, I found it all too easy to escape. Truly, I didn't love her. She had entered my life only because her sister, the one I had loved at first sight, had refused to disturb her studies for me. The nineteen-year-old Anna had not cared—she accepted my presence in her life with little thought and even less emotion. But as the youngest in their family, she became demanding, grasping at whatever she could, pulling me deeper into a life I never asked for. Maybe I was wrong for escaping. Maybe I was right. But all I knew was the overwhelming dissatisfaction gnawing at my insides, the constant weight of regret and confusion. I couldn't shake it, no matter how far I hid.

Back in the room, the footsteps reappeared, lingering outside the door. I listened intently, my pulse quickening, but I was determined not to open it. The louder I pretended to snore, the louder the knock persisted, as if taunting me.

"May I come in?" A familiar voice broke the silence.

"Who is it?" I asked, trying to sound indifferent, though my heart was racing.

"Anna," she answered.

"Anna, who?" I responded; my voice colder than I meant it to be.

With a sigh, I reluctantly opened the door. And there she stood—Anna Adzafunika Phiri, my wife. Awkward, strangely quiet, and somehow barren of warmth, yet gifted with a voice so angelic it almost made me falter. She had followed me here, and had invaded the fragile peace I had been clinging to. I sat on the edge of the bed, feeling a cold distance, while she knelt near the door, her posture a mix of humility and defiance.

"I am happy I've found you," Anna said, her voice a soft whisper. "I won't take much of your time. I've been thinking about what I should tell you before I leave your house." She paused, hesitating for a moment. "But you were quick to leave."

I stared at her sternly, my chin in my hand, my frustration bubbling just beneath the surface.

"I think you have forgotten what we did in the past. I don't think it's right for me to leave you," she continued, her voice faltering slightly. "But you insist…"

"Yes, I insist. Just leave me alone," I snapped, the words escaping before I could stop them, the weight of everything I felt pressing down on me.

She was quiet, and I noticed a watery substance trickling from her nose. Then, a sorrowful cry in a voice that seemed to carry the weight of silent suffering or perhaps deep annoyance escaped her lips. I pivoted my neck, straining to listen, as she cried.

After some time, she coughed.

I removed my hand from my chin, the meaning of her cough finally piercing through the fog of my frustration.

"I must tell you," she said, her voice trembling slightly. "You have no right to either leave me or tell me to leave your house. Do you forget what we buried together under the bed?"

I stared at her, the realization settling in. Her gaze met mine, and in that moment, all the fleeting thoughts of replacing her with someone new felt ridiculous. Unlike my first wife, Anna had kept my secrets, even when I didn't deserve it. A lump rose in my throat, and before I could stop myself, tears slipped down my cheeks.

Suddenly, I lunged forward, pulling her into a tight embrace, but she pulled away swiftly, racing towards the door. I dashed after her, my heart pounding, slicing through the cold air, desperate to catch her before she disappeared.

"Anna! Anna, please! Stop. Let's talk. It was just a joke."

Ahead of me, she scurried past the gate, her footsteps fading into the night. I watched helplessly as she fled into the darkness. From behind me, the wind howled, its cold fingers gripping my face, and I heard the mocking echoes of her retreating footsteps, laughing at my futile pursuit.

She was not supposed to reach the house before I did. If she removed what we buried, I would be finished. Panic tightened around my chest as I ran as fast as I could, dashing past large houses, each step heavier than the last, knowing I had to reach home before she did.

Then, just ahead, I heard footsteps—familiar, yet not quite. They reminded me of Anna's, but this wasn't her. These were the footsteps of strangers, the quick, purposeful tread of men closing in on me. My heart raced as I turned sharply, the air thickening with dread. They called out to me, their voices low and urgent, speaking of a woman who had ended her life behind the hotel. "Do you know her?" they asked, their words slicing through the night, pulling at something deep within me.

I froze for a moment, and the world collapsed around me. They stood there, the strange men, their eyes searching mine, and in that moment, I realized I wasn't running from Anna. I was running from something much darker, a mistake I couldn't undo.

Stranger in Her Own Skin

It was very early in the morning, and the air was thick with cheerful chorus of birds. The birds flitted from tree to tree, while their wings fluttered with excitement. The birds sang melodies that intended to celebrate the beauty of the dawn. Immediately, I woke up. This was an unusual day because I had to meet Thanda in Ntcheu, with full awareness that this would be the most sensational meeting. The birds' songs filled me with a sense of urgency, an indication that the trip was indeed very important. I had prepared for this moment, because it was the only chance I would get after several attempts. Thanda, my youngest sister, had sworn never to see my face again, and it had been a month since she announced this. Now this was an opportunity. I did not want to figure out what had occurred to her to invite me this time.

As I prepared myself, a wave of unexpected realization washed over me. I suddenly understood that anyone, at any moment, could make a decision that would change their life forever, especially after being touched by the right words. I felt a deep truth settling in—that words, when spoken with love, have the power to shift a person's heart. But the most surprising discovery of all was that change doesn't come from advice or encouragement alone; it comes from the willingness to change, the openness of the heart. The desire to transform, I realized, is more powerful than any comforting words a counsellor can offer.

Thanda's reasoning was less focused. I would say she was not determined to achieve more than we did. Most of the things she trusted was based on the circumstances that surrounded her. She was a girl who could not believe in dreams. Not just the dreams that shimmered in the jungle of sleep, but in the kind of magic that stirs deep in the soul—hope that never extinguishes, no matter how dark the night. She was the kind of person who could not see potential in everything, who could not believe that in the harshest trials, a glimmer of light could guide an individual through. To her, life was a test—a force that pushed and pulled, broke and remade, and the best thing to outsmart such challenges was to stay away from school, roam the streets, eat and drink what was offered by strangers. And smoke too.

Thanda, guided by misfortune, invited me. It was not just a random misfortune; it was the kind of tragedy that walked into people's life uninvited and changed everything. The misfortune had come to us—our family. And Thanda, my sister, was the one who bore the burden of it. This was why the meeting was called for. It was like watching a storm consume the essential part of her being, leaving the family members standing there, helpless, as Thanda became a stranger in her own skin.

I remember her laughing it off, though she had withered away to almost nothing. As she walked towards me, in her new frail frame, I was struck by the unshakable resolve that burned within her. It was as if her very soul was refusing to surrender, even as her body battled to survive.

Thanda refused to let the fear in her eyes define her. She lived among us, laughed with us, and shared her stories with us. She ate, she slept, she sang—the only unusual aspect of her life was her solitary meals, a habit that had earned her a reputation for being eccentric.

She did what she knew best. There were times that fear gripped her, especially when her friends forced her to explain what had happened. There was nothing she could do but smile, laugh, and blend in with the crowd, as if everything was normal, though every act of joy felt like it was eating her from within. She had to, from deep within her heart. There was no other way. She was strong—she had to be. She had to speak, to laugh, above all to appear unbroken.

She lived like this for a long time, her body surviving on little food, drinking copious amounts of water, injecting herself with insulin, and surrendering to the frequent embrace of sleep. From the outside, she seemed fragile, her pain almost palpable in the hollow beneath her eyes and the slight tremble of her hands. But she assured me that the pain was not as consuming as it appeared. What stung even more was the revelation that many of her friends had been talking about her condition in hushed tones, exaggerating it as if it were a death sentence. They claimed she had little time left, that her situation was somehow a consequence of reckless choices she made in her youth. She longed to explain, to reveal the quiet torment she carried, but it was difficult. So many of her friends were too young, too naive to understand the complexity of her struggle. She let them mock her, gossip about her, dismiss her pain with laughter and careless words. She let them think what they would.

*****

Thanda, the youngest in our family, had always been a radiant and enchanting presence, from birth till she entered primary school, until something shattered her innocence. I remember feeling the change in her as soon as she entered a boarding secondary school in Ndirande. It was during the very first week of the first-term holiday that she suddenly displayed strange behaviour. I sensed something was wrong. I could feel that she had experimented with 'weed.' When I confronted her, she hesitantly admitted it and tearfully blamed the senior girls, who pressured every student to taste it. The news hit us like a thunderclap. My brother, Thom and I immediately took action, reporting the incident to the headteacher, who vowed to address it promptly and expel the ringleaders. Together, we urged Thanda to stand strong and report anyone who tried to coerce her into smoking. We worked tirelessly to protect her from the dogged grip of peer pressure, determined not to let it swallow her.

However, our efforts bore little fruit. This we understood when we packed her school fees in between her books and instructed her to pay once she reached the school premises. Thanda spent it on shoes and outfits for a mock wedding—a shocking revelation I only learned after her headteacher informed me that her term two fees were unpaid. As I frantically negotiated a late payment for term three, the truth slammed into me like a harsh slap to the face. I couldn't process it at first. But when I confronted Thanda in front of her headteacher and the school director, she admitted it without a trace of remorse. That moment marked the death of my trust in her. Her words had turned into a landfill of lies, filled with half-truths and manipulations.

Thom, however, had little patience left for her. He accused Thanda of stealing his money, and at first, I dismissed it as another misunderstanding. But when I found her flaunting new clothes and shoes, my doubts crystallized into certainty. We had tried everything—counselling, urging her to stay in school, hoping she would finally grasp the importance of securing her future. But

Thanda was beyond repair. She was a storm, untamable and wild, listening only to her own voice. No matter what we did, she could not be changed from the path she had chosen for herself.

Come October, we planned to send Thanda to a reformatory centre in Mpemba. Maybe after spending some time there, she would be trained to behave. We had called the authorities and registered her name. Just before picking her to Mpemba, Thanda suddenly fell sick. She called me one particular night inviting me to a meeting between Thom, myself and herself. It was around midnight, and her voice cut through the heavy fog of sleep that enveloped me. I knew she was a problem. Now, what was it?

My body was heavy and my mind thick with the remnants of a long day. The phone vibrated against my palm, and for a moment, I thought I might slip back into the abyss of sleep. But then, her voice broke through, fragile and desperate, and I managed to force out a hoarse, trembling "hello," the words slipping from me like water through trembling fingers. "It's me, Thanda. Can you hear me, Sue?" She speaks.

I felt the pull of her distress through the trembling strain in her voice. Something cold and unsettling crept into my mind, suggesting it might be just another clash between her and Thom. The same old cycle—misunderstandings about weed and theft. It had always been this way between them since it was discovered that she was listening to herself.

"What's going on there? Another quarrel with Thom?"

"No. Something strange." She uttered.

The line went dead, and the silence hung there, thick and suffocating.

I called her back. The anticipation in my chest felt like the slow burn of a flame.

"Get to the point, please." I exclaimed.

"If you can manage to travel to Brother Thom's place, please, check up on me. I am not well."

Her reply was like a cold gust of wind. The words left me reeling, their significance hitting me with overwhelming force. Silence stretched again, but I knew she was there, somewhere in that dark space, listening. I ended the call abruptly.

I knew Thanda was lost—so much of her life had unravelled. The big sign was that she had turned into an average student, yet she had been a shining star in primary school. But she was my sister, and at that moment, I knew my role. I would hold space for her weaknesses. I would forgive her a thousand times over if it meant she might find her way back to herself. No matter how broken or misbehaved she seemed, there was no bin where I could throw her away. She was my blood. And I could not be the one to let her slip through the cracks of my life without offering my hand. The thought of not being there for her when she needed me filled me with dread—regret was a mountain I could not climb. So, I made my choice. I would do my part, while I still had the chance to be there for her.

Sleep eluded me that night. Restlessness consumed me, urging me to make a decision. I resolved to take a drive, even if it meant

41

venturing into the darkness. It was only an hour's drive to Ntcheu, and I could return to Balaka by morning. I called Thom to let him know my plans. He hesitated for a moment, though his voice was thick with concern, but he encouraged me not to travel that night.

But that night, my mind was not just on the road. It was on Thanda—the girl whose life had become a constant source of confusion and worry. No one in the family believed what had happened to her. If there was ever a girl who should have thrived with education, it was Thanda. Everything was handed to her. Yet, she lacked the hunger for knowledge, the drive to succeed. Her laziness seemed to seep into her every action, and it was this that compelled me to intervene, time and again, in her stupidity.

I realized that I had not slept until 5:00 a.m. I started off. I could not accept that Thanda should die at such a young age. No matter what it was. No matter what spell was cast upon her. She might have exaggerated it in order to milk money for her extravagant life, but as my sister I had to ensure that she was safe. It was obvious Thom was tired of her lies and whatever she did to him was rubbish. Of course, she was a profligate but my sister, she remained. Her blood was my blood. Her roots were my roots. Her graveyard would be my graveyard. If Thanda told me that she had not long to live, I knew there was something serious.

Around 6:30 a.m. I met Thom. He greeted me and led me to Thanda's room. She was drained and weak. I asked Thom to leave us alone for a moment.

"Are you sick or there's something more than sickness that is eating you up?" I asked her, immediately.

"I am always hungry and thirsty. But that is not a big issue. Come close, Sue. Check the wound at my back. Sister, I am in trouble."

I removed her bedsheets and switched on the lights. A big wound gaped at me. I at once hid my face. A tear fell on the floor. Another one on my arm.

"Sue, I am dying."

She excused herself and rose up to pass out urine. As she walked, it was like a skeleton was moving. On return, she asked for water to drink before munching a piece of bread.

I walked out to meet Thom. He was not interested in discussing her matters, but he told me her appearance had changed in the space of four days. The sad part was that she was not telling him what was wrong. I told him what I saw, and advised that Thanda had to be checked by the doctor.

Immediately, we started off, to Ntcheu District Hospital. Different thoughts bombarded me from every direction. Above all was the fact that we could not let her die because she was a dunderhead. We could not let her die because she was a thief. We could not let her die because she did not want to listen to us. We could not aid her death by abandoning her. We had to accept her as our problem. We could not treat her as a stranger. I whispered my thoughts to Thom, and he nodded his head.

When we met the doctor, she approved of multiple tests. All the other tests were negative except the blood sugar. A smile walked on her face when finally, the doctor said the wound could not heal because of nothing, but rising blood sugar levels. People living with diabetes had problems with wounds. "I will help you to lower the blood sugar levels and the wound will heal," the doctor muttered.

When we reached home, Thanda opened her mouth.

"Brother and sister, I know I have often let you down. I am far from perfect, and I carry the load of my mistakes with me every day. But something that Sue said to you, brother, before we went to the hospital, really touched my heart. She spoke of your support for me, no matter how much I have failed you, simply because I am your sister. Her words brought tears to my eyes, and I couldn't help but feel the deep sadness of all I have done wrong. I have hurt you both in ways you never deserved. I have taken from you, betrayed your trust, and acted selfishly, all in pursuit of my own desires. Please, forgive me for the pain I have caused.

It's true I am your sister. I want you to know that from today, my story will be different. I have decided to change. I am facing a battle—one that I cannot fight alone. I have been diagnosed with diabetes, and this time, I need your support more than ever. I'm asking for your understanding, your help, and your love. I am determined to rise above this, to make the most of this second chance, and to show you that I can be better. I will excel in my studies, not only to honour my own journey, but to honour the sacrifices you've made for me. Your support means a lot to me."

Listening to Thanda, all of us broke down. Tears of both joy and sadness snaked down our cheeks ceaselessly. It was her courage, her raw boldness to speak so openly, that cracked us wide open. Her words, painted with painful wisdom gained far too soon, paralysed us with sorrow. We weren't just crying for her—we were pleading with the Almighty God to heal her, to protect her, to guide her back to school, and to help her fight for the future she deserved. She assured us, with quiet determination that she would. We smiled through the tears, in total agreement with that spark of hope she gave us. She stood tall, unbroken, and even as the world seemed to cast its cruelest shadows on those living with non-communicable diseases, diseases that slowly and steadily steal life away. Her strength, in the face of such unimaginable challenges, left us humbled, grieving, and awestruck.

I returned back to Balaka overwhelmed with a sense of joy and gratitude. My heart felt light, and a wave of happiness enveloped me as I reflected on the meeting. It had been more than just successful—it had been transformative, a turning point for Thanda that I hadn't fully anticipated. Before leaving, I waved at Thanda. She waved back at me, confidently.

Beyond Personal Wishes

The sun's rays kissed the earth that October noon with a great intensity of heat. I had just come home for lunch when Madala called me. He had that tendency of calling me when he had a burning issue to be discussed—and he did that without following proper protocols—in most cases, he would start with a chorus.

"My son, don't be so quick to assume that life is better elsewhere," Madala cautioned, his eyes scrutinizing mine as if to ensure I was truly listening. "Life is what you've experienced, how you've chosen to view it, and how you think you can turn things around."

He paused, studying me intently, as if to gauge my comprehension. His words were a response to my earlier declaration that I couldn't survive in the tropical African country, my country, plagued as it was by a multitude of problems—lack of employment, poor healthcare, and a host of other issues. I had expressed my desire to leave for South Africa, hoping to find better luck.

Madala's expression turned stern. "How can I pay for your travel documents when I haven't given you my blessing to leave?" he asked, his tone firm but well calculated. "If you're determined to go, make your own plans. Save money from your internships and go alone. If you encounter problems, that's when I'll step in to help you return. But I want you to try your luck here, put your motherland first."

I did not reply. I left the place to take the food warmer and gluttonously fingered my food. Without attending to what Masiteni was saying, I went back to my place of work, Zilindiiwe Private School, where I was doing my internship soon after finishing university education.

As I wandered through the village path, I couldn't shake the feeling that my current life was suffocating me. I was too tired. The desires of my youth - including financial stability, a good music system, a sleek car, and a comfortable home - seemed impossible to attain while doing such a menial job. Madala had always known that I had bigger aspirations. I fought for it. I worked hard in school. I got a good grade. However, I could not find a permanent job. I felt an overwhelming urge to break free from the constraints of my current life.

As I walked, I had made up my mind to take a leap of faith and try my luck elsewhere. Since Madala had rebuffed my proposal, I mentally prepared myself for the conversation I wanted to have with the school director. I would ask him for a small loan which I could use for the processing fees of my passport. I was willing to work for two terms without pay if it meant achieving my goal. My determination to leave behind the familiar - my parents, my country, and everything that distracted me from my path to success - burned stronger as days multiplied into weeks, and weeks into months. I groped for freedom, wealth, and a life that was unfettered by the limitations of my current existence. I knew I would get it. I had to leave Madala alone with his views that I described as filled with concoctions of backwardness, views that would take youthful and energetic minds nowhere.

Thirty minutes later, I stood outside the school director's office, my heart racing with anticipation. I took a deep breath, raised my hand, and knocked on the door. The wait seemed interminable, but finally, after two minutes, I heard the sound of papers shuffling and the director's voice bidding me enter.

As I stepped inside, I poured out my heart, sharing the dreams and desires that had been burning within me for so long. I needed the director's help, for I knew that my father, for reasons unknown, had failed to provide the support I craved.

The director listened intently, his eyes narrowing as he adjusted his glasses. After a thoughtful pause, he spoke. "Meet me again tomorrow, and we'll discuss the details." I nodded my head, my mind racing with possibilities, and left the office.

Back home, I was met with an unsettling silence. Madala's gaze followed me as I walked towards my room, his eyes dissecting me with a mixture of disappointment and resignation. It was clear that he sensed my growing detachment from the life we had built together. There were no two ways about it. I had spent the better part of my youth within these walls, but the familiarity now felt stifling. I yearned for independence, for the freedom to forge my own path and create a life that was truly mine. The desire to make a name for myself, to accumulate wealth, and to build a family of my own had become an all-consuming passion.

But I knew that these dreams would remain elusive as long as I remained tied to my parents' expectations. Their interests, though well-intentioned, were no longer aligned with mine. It was time for me to prioritize my own needs, to put my own desires first. I had to go away. I had to make life for myself.

That evening, I retired to my room without exchanging a word with anyone. The silence was oppressive, but I knew it was necessary.

I was drawing a line, marking the beginning of a new chapter in my life. And I was ready to face whatever lay ahead, alone. Enough was enough. They couldn't treat me like a baby all the days of my life.

The night stretched out before me while my mind was racing with anticipation. Tomorrow, I would hear from the director, and my fate would be sealed. As I lay flat, my thoughts wandered to the struggles of my peers. Did they, like me, feel suffocated by the weight of their parents' expectations?

I pondered the delicate balance between parental support and independence. Were parents not doing enough to prepare their children for the real world? Were they instead creating a culture of dependency, where children expected their parents to solve all their problems?

The examples were countless–parents finding jobs for their grown children, sponsoring their weddings, and even providing for their grandchildren. It was as if the parents' responsibility never ended. But at what cost? I had seen it time and time again: parents sacrificing their own well-being, their own happiness, to provide for their children.

Just as my thoughts were starting to unravel, the cock in the neighbour's house let out a loud crow. I jolted awake, the sound piercing the darkness. I threw off the blanket and began to prepare for the day ahead, writing lesson plans and filling the schemes and records of work, my mind still reeling with the weight of my own decisions.

As I stepped into the school director's office, a mix of exhaustion and optimism swirled within me. The previous night's anticipation had taken its toll, but I was determined to face whatever lay ahead. The school director, seated behind his desk, waved me in with a curt gesture. His expression was open, yet his words were laced with a hint of warning.

"My job is to keep my staff happy," he said, his voice firm but clear. "As an intern, you are not part of my staff. I just felt sorry when you said you wanted a job. There was no vacancy here." He leaned forward, his eyes locking onto mine.

I felt a surge of frustration at his response. Hadn't I made it clear that I wasn't asking for a handout? All I wanted was for him to give me my wages in advance and deduct me accordingly, and yet he was refusing. I couldn't help but wonder if the rumours about some bosses were true, that they were selfish and exploitative, only looking out for their own interests.

I rose from my seat, feeling a sense of disillusionment wash over me. Why stay with a boss who couldn't understand my situation? Had I made a mistake by revealing my plans to him? I left the office, the door swinging open behind me like an unanswered question.

I wandered aimlessly around the school compound, trying to clear my head and think of my next move. I couldn't believe that the director had been so unwilling to help me. Didn't he care about the well-being of his employees?

As I walked, I noticed one of my colleagues, watching me from across the compound. She was a kind and wise woman, and I had always valued her opinion. I walked over to her, hoping to find some guidance and support.

"Good morning, Madam," I said, trying to sound calm. "I just had a meeting with the director, and I'm feeling a bit frustrated. Do you notice?"

She looked at me with concern and asked, "What happened?"

I took a deep breath and told her everything - about my desire to leave the country, about my conversation with the director, and about my feelings of frustration and disappointment.

She listened attentively, nodding her head from time to time. When I finished speaking, she put a hand on my shoulder and said, "Don't worry, you are still young. You will find a way. Sometimes, we have to take risks and trust that everything will work out. Just go back and apologise. Tell him, you did it without investing much reason. You were not supposed to request for a loan. By the way, I will talk to a few teachers. Maybe, we can help with that small loan— and you will pay for your passport. Leave the director alone."

I listened very carefully and I saw that it was necessary to share my problems first with my colleagues instead of my boss.

That day, I went through the motions of providing teaching and learning aids, but my heart wasn't in it. The classroom was a blur of faces and distractions, and I found myself zoning out, lost in thought.

I would try to make a point, only to trail off, feeling like I was speaking to an empty room. The irony wasn't lost on me - I was trying to teach, but my own mind was elsewhere. At one point, I stopped mid-sentence, feeling the heaviness of my frustration. I couldn't shake the feeling that I was just going through the motions, that I was stuck in a rut. I didn't need anyone to tell me that I was off my game - I knew it myself.

The rest of the day was a haze. I skipped lunch, opting instead to sit alone in the staff room. When the final bell rang at 2:30 p.m., I gathered my things and headed straight home, collapsing onto my bed in exhaustion.

Madala tried to talk to me, but I shut him down, unable to face his questions or concerns. Masiteni knocked on my bedroom door, her gentle voice was but nice music to the turmoil brewing inside me. But I ignored her too, pulling the bed sheets over my head and letting the darkness hide me.

As I lay in bed, I couldn't shake off the feeling of restlessness that had been building up inside me. It was as if I was trapped in a prison of my own making, with no clear escape route in sight. The sound of my mother's knocking grew fainter, and I knew she had given up trying to rouse me. I felt a pang of guilt, knowing that she was worried about me, but I couldn't bring myself to face her.

As the night wore on, I found myself drifting in and out of consciousness, my mind racing with thoughts of my future. I knew I couldn't stay in this limbo forever, but I had no idea what the next step was.

It wasn't until the sound of cocks crowing pierced the darkness that I finally stirred. I threw off the bed sheets and got out of bed, my body stiff from a night of tossing and turning. As I made my way to the bathroom to wash my face, I caught a glimpse of myself in the mirror. My eyes were sunken, my skin pale. I was a shadow of my former self.

I took a deep breath and let the water run over my face, feeling a sense of determination wash over me. It was a new day, and I had to be myself. I had to rethink my plans. I had to make sure that I was the winner. My colleagues would help. I trusted them.

However, during the last week of August, my contract with Zilindiiwe Private School expired, and I had been holding onto a sliver of hope that it might not be renewed. Deep down, I knew it was a long shot, but a part of me had been clinging to the possibility of a fresh start.

On Thursday evening, at around 6:30 p.m., I received a call from a colleague who was close to the director. He told me he had a letter for me, and I could sense a hint of trepidation in his voice. I made myself stronger and agreed to meet him, my heart racing with hope.

As I approached him, I could see the forced smile on his face. He attempted to make light of the situation, but I could see the tension behind his eyes. I knew, without a doubt, that he was the bearer of bad news.

I took the letter from him, my hands trembling slightly as I opened the envelope. The words on the page seemed to blur together, but I knew what I was looking for. I scanned the letter quickly, my heart sinking as I read the words that would change everything.

I got it. My time with the institution was over. I embarked on a desperate quest to unravel the mystery behind the non-renewal of my contract. Had I been too candid about my plans to leave the country in search of better opportunities? Or had my performance been lacking, failing to meet the expectations of my director? The questions swirled in my mind, refusing to yield any clear answers.

As I walked down the road, lost in thought, I couldn't shake off the memory of the school director's gaze on the day I had requested him to withhold my salary. It had been a look of sadness, of disappointment, and perhaps even of anger. I wondered if that moment had been the turning point, the instant when my fate had been sealed.

Despite my best efforts to remain strong, I felt a lump form in my throat as the reality of my situation began to sink in. Tears pricked at the corners of my eyes, and I felt a stinging sensation as they began to flow, snaking down my cheeks like rivulets of sorrow. I didn't bother to wipe them away, letting them fall instead, a testament to the pain and uncertainty that had taken up residence in my heart. I had to be strong, I told myself. I had to believe that I was able to do great things. I swore that my situation would reverse for the better.

I collapsed onto my bed, tired and emotionally drained. I needed a moment to collect myself before breaking the news to Madala. I wiped away my tears, knowing that he would demand answers, not emotions. Madala was a man who thrived on logic and reason, always seeking to understand the why behind every event. I would need to be prepared to explain what had happened, how I had failed to prevent it, and what I planned to do next.

As I lay in bed, my mind began to wander. If I wanted to fund my trip abroad, I would need to attach myself as an intern in a certain organization. But where? The new academic calendar was just around the corner, and all the nearby schools had already hired new staff and distributed resources. I knew that the director of Zilindiiwe Private School had deliberately sabotaged my chances, wanting me to suffer for my decision to leave. But I refused to give up. I believed that when one door closed, another would always open, no matter how long it took.

As the cocks began to sing, I finally felt ready to face Madala. I waited till the sun rose to a good length.

"Madala, we need to talk," I said, trying to sound calm and confident.

My father looked up at me, his eyes narrowing slightly as he took in my expression. "What's going on?" he asked, his voice firm but concerned.

I took a deep breath and launched into the story, telling him everything that had happened with the school director and the non-renewal of my contract. I explained how my plans had been thwarted and that there was no way I would fulfil my dream.

As I spoke, I could see the tension in Madala's body begin to ease. He listened attentively, his eyes never leaving mine, and when I finished, he nodded thoughtfully.

"I'm proud of you," he said, his voice filled with emotion. "I have admired your fighting spirit, your will to do well. Now I am convinced you are a visionary man. I have been hiding the truth for a long time. Tomorrow, you must get ready to go and pay for your passport. There is a scholarship for you that my sister is facilitating. You will be going to America next month."

I felt a wind of gratitude towards Madala, and I shed tears of joy before hugging him.

Trapped

The sour smell of remorse coiled around me as a familiar white car blinked outside. My stomach roiled in disgust. The heat in my chest burned hotter than the sting of unshed tears. I gasped, disbelief and anger warring within me.

I figured out immediately that Aunt Maya had played some tricks. Her voice like a rusty saw dragging through the bone had ripped through my carefully constructed story. I was finished!

Earlier, I had envisioned a friendly welcome. I had dreamt of her frail hand squeezing mine, a silent promise that together, we would weave a mantle of secrecy around the solution that was yet to bloom. But as I found her, I discovered that she had changed completely—both physically and morally—such that her steel-trap gaze immediately pinned me to the floor.

"Let me repeat. I said I have come," I choked out, the carefully rehearsed words dissolving in the acid of her gaze of dissatisfaction. A lump, the size of a tomato, lodged in my throat.

"Don't think I haven't thought about the purpose of your visit," she spat, each word a spike of ice. "I have already seen you. Just stand up! Don't kneel as though you are a real girl!"

Aunt Maya barked. As her eyes met mine, I looked down. I banked on her to help me, but now here I was being greeted with a basketfull of admonition. I thought it was a well-thought-of plan such that I would get positive feedback, a position I seriously looked forward to.

"I have come," I gathered my strength again to speak, but I stopped to swallow saliva.

"Stop it." She cut my statement with a sharp-razored-mouth, and waved to me to keep quiet.

The day did not start well. It curdled in my stomach long before dawn. As I rose, I felt like a lead weight was tethered to my limbs. I felt a familiar urge to expel something like bile in my throat. I swallowed it back, its acrid taste mirroring the souring of my carefully laid plans.

By five o'clock in the morning, I was at the bus stop in Zomba. Two and a half hours stretched before me. I had to meet Aunt Maya in the village. I told myself. Aunt Maya had married with a laugh that could light up a room—and stayed in Mangani village.

As I started off, I figured out that I would find not only peace, but a lifeline thrown from the wreckage of my own choices.

I alighted from the bus at New Stage, and coincidentally met a young boy who was curious with my face. I snubbed him, adjusted my sun glasses and put my laptop bag at the back. Doubtless that I was taking the right direction, I attuned the ear phones to listen to my favourite song while descending the hills into Mangani village that was situated in the valley.

As the path meandered through rocks providing a clear view of the village, unlike in my previous visits, I saw a lot of iron-roofed houses. Memories of how I climbed that hill after Aunt Maya's wedding ceremony a few years ago were still fresh in my mind. That time, the path was hidden by fresh tall grass which the villagers used to harvest for thatching their houses and mounting fences around their homes. As I strolled half way down the path, adjacent to the source of Mafisi River, there was a long zigzagging stretch of bamboo that housed baboons. Walking in the corridor of darkness created by the bamboo, I wouldn't see the grass roofs of the houses in the valley until I reached the end of the path which had a lot of grass too.

But now the whole hill was shaved naked and the corrugated iron sheets had descended into the village. At that point, I was able to see and count up to fifty iron-roofed houses.

Eating the distance slowly, I noticed that the strange boy was following me. He was carrying a box of matches, five yellow buns and salt wrapped in a clear plastic paper. As he walked closely behind me, there was a strange ordour which I felt was coming from him. He looked like he had not taken a bath for several days—and the very fact that he was bare and his hair was unkempt, I thought he had a mental problem. Looking over my shoulders, he smiled at me as a gesture of recognition, but I did not identify him. I once in a while visited my home village and such experiences were expected. I stopped, performing a show of flipping through clothes in my bag as if looking for something important, to check whether the boy would pass me by or not. In a moment, I figured out that the boy had stopped too, and was scampering into the remnants of the bush. I thought about walking very fast to leave him behind, but the thought stopped in its tracks. I could not wait to reach Aunt Maya's house before I talked to him in case something happened to me. This was my home village where relationships mattered.

Contrary to my fears, the boy whispered to me, "I am Joab, Aunt Maya's first-born son. Trinity, your name is Trinity." He exclaimed.

"Yes. You are right. I am Trinity."

"Would you mind if I carry your bag?" Joab offered.

"It is not very heavy. Thank you so much." I refused.

"How is James, your young brother?"

"He is just okay, doing fine in standard five."

"I am also doing fine in standard one. My teacher told me to repeat. Now I am a master."

"In which class are you?" Joab asked.

"I am at the university in Zomba. Year 2."

Happiness surged through me. I trailed behind Joab, my eyes glued to his eager strides as he raced to share the news of my surprise visit with Aunt Maya.

A desperate need to return to my home village, to seek refuge in Aunt Maya's embrace, consumed me. The weight of my secret, a silent, festering wound, grew heavier with each passing moment. I longed for her wisdom, her strength, to guide me through the darkness I was in. The decision was clear: the unwanted life within me had to be terminated. I had to be free, and hide everything from my father, who was the only surviving parent and a lover of books.

My father had three huge problems: asthma, high blood pressure and diabetes. I could not be the fourth one.

Upon seeing me, a flicker of recognition passed over Aunt Maya's face. Her eyes, usually brimming with warmth, held a cold, distant gaze. She had read my mind.

"Sit on the mat, and look at me. Am I happy?" Her voice was a harsh whisper.

"Everyone knows you are not," I replied, my own voice trembling slightly.

"I am not," she confirmed, her tone flat. "I was a child when they said I should marry. They took my innocence, forced me into a life of dependence. So, you want to join me and my party?" Her words were like needles, piercing through my heart.

"No. I do not. That's why I want to remove it," I managed to say, my voice barely audible.

"Year 2 undergraduate! You are still so young and so foolish," she scoffed. Her dismissal—a heavy blow, a cold slap to my face.

I shed bitter tears, but a flicker of hope ignited within me. Aunt Maya, with her wrinkled hands and knowing eyes, had to possess some herbal potion or sacred ritual to rectify this terrible wrong. She would know what to do.

"Look at me. In my youth, I thought love and sex were important," Aunt Maya continued after a long silence, her voice a low, rumbling echo in the quiet room. "I wasted precious years chasing fleeting passions. Now, I understand the cruel dance of time and consequence. You see me as a fallen woman, yet you dare to ask me to undo the mistakes of your generation. I cannot be your saviour, your magic healer. Go to the clinic!"

Her words were like thorns, piercing my already wounded heart.

"I do not have the courage," I whispered, my voice barely audible.

"And who inflicted this shame upon you?" Aunt Maya demanded, her voice rising.

"Thoko," I replied, the name tasting like pepper on my lips.

"That reckless neighbour," she spat, her voice thick with contempt. "A walking plague, spreading disease like wildfire."

I shivered. A cold dread crept down my spine. The image of Thoko flashed before my eyes.

"But you used to say circumcised men were smart men," I mumbled, my voice trembling. She did not reply.

I looked at Aunt Maya, her voice was a rough screech in the oppressive silence. The choking scent of her natural perfume seemed to thicken the atmosphere. It was a suffocating presence painting the long years of suffering she had endured. Since she had vowed not to help me, the heavy weight of despair pressed down on my chest, and I fled the room, straight to the toilet.

The floor and walls of the toilet seemed to mock my misery. A cold draft whistled through the small opening designed to be a window, chilling my skin as I pulled a rope from my trouser pocket.

The best solution was not only to kill the foetus, but myself too. The texture of the rope was smooth against my fingers, a necessary weapon to wipe out my presence from the world. However, the pressure of the rope against my throat was suffocating, a physical manifestation of the emotional stranglehold I felt, and the pain that blossomed was deeper than the physical discomfort. I couldn't do it. I went back to the room.

At around 7pm I asked for a mat to sleep on. Just then, a nightmare clawed its way into my consciousness. There was a distant roar of engines piercing the silence. A cold sweat broke out as I tried to flee the approaching cavalcade of cars. The blinding lights of the cars seemed to bore into my skull. Trapped in their eerie circle, I was a helpless prey. I cried as the touch of a strange woman's hand in the dream was rough. Her grip tightened. Pain exploded within me. The metallic tang of blood filled my senses as I saw it splatter. I jolted awake while my heart was pounding like a frantic drum.

The house was dark and silent, save for the soft creak of the door. The cool night air was a refreshing slap to my face as I slipped outside. Just then, the gleam of my father's car cut through the darkness. My father! Regret like a bitter taste in my mouth washed over me. I heard him talking to Aunt Maya behind the car. My name was in his mouth. I immediately felt that Aunt Maya's betrayal was like a concrete slab, aimed at sealing my fate. I vowed I couldn't meet my father. A bag slung over my shoulder; I ran towards New Stage.

As I jogged, the thinking about Aunt Maya's betrayal burned worse than the squeeze on my stomach. My escape route, the moonlit hill, stretched before me, but a new fear snagged at my breath. What if the cavalcade of cars and everything I saw in the nightmare were waiting for me at the top?

I moved on. The following day, Zomba Bus Depot welcomed me. The weight of my bag felt like an anchor as I dragged it up while the harsh sunlight reflecting off the university campus buildings into my eyes. A cacophony of familiar voices and laughter swirled around me like a cyclone of noise that threatened to drown out my own pounding heart. This was it. The start of a new life. I had told myself. But as I glanced back at the fading image of my village and all that happened, a cold dread seeped into my bones. Wild thoughts raced through my mind. Freedom, adventure, escape - these were the dreams I had clung to. But now, a different reality was looming, a secret that felt like a ticking time bomb. My father's phone message popped few minutes after my escape. It was a desperate plea to make me understand that such was life. I should not worry too much, and the best solution was to have a child, not to terminate it. The message replayed in my mind. The words had a different tone to his usually stern demeanor, and they chilled me to the core. I had to heed his advice, though I knew his decision had not come easily. It could be the efforts of Aunt Maya. I thought avoidance would be my shield as a way to protect myself from the storm of emotions that were threatening to engulf me. But I had to think twice and follow the route of acceptance.

Nine months later, a smile walked on my face. A tiny boy was placed in my arms. His first cry, such a raw and powerful sound, echoed through Zomba Central Hospital. I named him Blessings, a hopeful name for a future shrouded in uncertainty. My father, with a strength I had not known he possessed, stepped up to raise the boy. He did it, with love that was both fierce and tender. Aunt Maya used to bring gifts of clothes for him—and Blessings thrived. His laughter filled the home.

Years passed, and my life took a different path. I finished my studies and got a steady job at the National Bank. I also got a loving husband, and everything seemed perfect. Yet, there was something that was missing –a longing gnawed at me, a void that no career or companionship could fill. I needed another child, and many years passed, without a new baby on my lap. It was only Blessings, the boy I had nearly relinquished to the world, who became the only child that warmed my house.

The Road to Chiweta

I stood at the edge of the road that brought me to Chiweta. My eyes were fixed upon a vista that held me captive. The sun splashed its golden hues upon the undulating surface of Lake Malawi, transforming it into shimmering curtains of molten fire. Every ripple was a dance of light, a symphony of colors that stirred the depths of my soul. The imposing Boliwoli hills in Rumphi District, majestic and steadfast, stood like mighty guards, their verdant peaks brushing against the heavens as if guarding nature's most treasured sanctuary.

The Kamchacha-Chiweta road was my first product after my Civil Engineering Degree at The Polytechnic, the University of Malawi, a testament to my unwavering passion and meticulous craftsmanship. It was a 96.4 km road that embraced the hills with tender grace, like a lover's caress, guiding all who ventured upon it to the shores of this enchanted lake. The 2h 19 min road itself was an artwork, its twists and turns a testimony to the harmonious marriage of human ingenuity and the raw beauty of the land. It was my masterpiece, a manifestation of my vision brought to life.

As I stood there, basking in the radiance of the sun's golden embrace, I couldn't help but feel a surge of pride swelling within my chest. The road breathed with a vitality all its own, a living artery that connected the distant horizons, beckoning adventurers and dreamers alike to traverse its winding path to see the lake at Mlowe. It was more than mere asphalt and gravel; it was a conduit of possibilities, a bridge between worlds waiting to be discovered.

At that moment, I felt a profound sense of fulfillment. The road I had designed had become more than just a means of transportation. It was a gateway to beauty, to serenity, to a realm where nature's wonders unfolded like an ethereal ballet. Each stone placed with precision, every curve shaped with intention, had forged a connection between humanity and the breathtaking drapes that stretched before us.

I marveled at the symphony of nature and human creation, intertwined in perfect harmony. The vibrant dance of sunlight upon the lake mirrored the spark of inspiration that had ignited within me during the road's inception. It was a fusion of artistry and the grandeur of the natural world, forever etched into the tapestry of my existence.

As the wind whispered through the trees and the distant echoes of birdsongs caressed my ears, I knew that this road held a promise. A promise of exploration, of boundless discovery, and of everlasting memories waiting to be woven into the fabric of time. It was not just a road, but a vessel of dreams, inviting all who ventured upon it to immerse themselves in the breathtaking embrace of nature's splendor.

With a heart brimming with gratitude, I lingered for a moment longer, drinking in the beauty that surrounded me. The sun's golden rays kissed my face, and I knew that my creation had found its rightful place in the world, nestled within the embrace of hills and the embrace of this enchanting lake.

When I had designed and built this road, an overwhelming surge of pride flowed through my veins, as if I had become a sculptor of the land, shaping the very essence of the landscape to mirror my vision. With each curve and bend, I breathed life into the earth, molding the road to dance in perfect synchrony with the undulating beauty that enveloped it. It was a labor of love that demanded nothing less than the fragments of my heart and soul, meticulously woven into every inch of its existence. Like an artist wielding a brush, I delicately blended the road into nature's canvas, ensuring that it seamlessly harmonized with the surrounding shades of serenity and wonder. The mere thought of connecting people to this oasis ignited a fire of immeasurable joy within me as if I held the key to a realm of tranquility waiting to be unlocked.

With tireless dedication, I poured my passion into the very asphalt that now kissed the earth's surface. Each curve was a brushstroke, every bend a stroke of genius.

As I stood at the road's completion, surveying my masterpiece, I could almost hear the whispers of the hills and the murmurs of the lake, expressing their gratitude for the pathway that now wound through their midst. It was as if I had breathed life into dormant veins, infusing the land with the pulse of connectivity, inviting travelers to embark on a pilgrimage to this serene haven.

The road became a peculiar bridge, spanning the realms of possibility and beckoning wanderers to traverse its winding path. It was a thread of unity, weaving communities together and sewing the embroidery of shared experiences. Like a river, it flowed seamlessly, carving its way through the hills and leading travelers to the enchantment that awaited them at the water's edge.

In the depths of my soul, I reveled in the realization that my creation had become more than just a road. It was a conduit of dreams, a gateway to the sublime. I had birthed a pathway of transcendence, where the mundane and the extraordinary intertwined, and where ordinary lives could be touched by the wonders of this world.

Years have passed, only half of a decade and my soul yearns to feast its eyes on the magnificence of my creation. I long to gaze at the beauty of the glittering midnight black asphalt in those majestic hills.

But now, back to my stroke of genius, as I stood once again at the road's threshold, disappointment clawed at my heart. Time had taken its toll, and the road bore the scars of neglect. Like a fading masterpiece left to weather the passage of years, cracks marred its surface, and the echoes of the past began to fade. It pained me to witness the gradual erosion of its magnificence like a melody slowly fading into the realm of forgotten whispers.

The once vibrant brushstrokes that embraced the hills now wore the shroud of weariness, and the road's connection to the lake seemed fractured as if a precious bond had been severed. My heart ached with the weight of a thousand lost opportunities, wondering if this road, my road, would ever be restored to its former glory.

Hope flickered within me, a fragile flame yearning to be nurtured. I longed for the day when the road would rise from its slumber, revived and rejuvenated, ready to carry the dreams of future generations. But uncertainty gnawed at the edges of my optimism, casting a shadow over the possibility of an upgrade, leaving me adrift in a sea of doubt.

I vividly remember the day I presented my project to the 1965 August House. Their eyes widened with awe as I unveiled the plans and outlined my vision. They applauded as I spoke passionately about the road's potential to boost tourism, bring economic growth, and provide a gateway for countless visitors to experience the wonders of this breathtaking place.

Standing here now, my heart sank with a deep sense of disappointment. The road was in disrepair, marred by potholes and faded lane markings. It was a stark contrast to the grandeur it once exuded. It was as if time had eroded not only the asphalt but also the dreams I had poured into its creation.

I felt a knot tighten in my chest as I realized that the road may never receive the attention it deserved. The prospect of an upgrade, a restoration of its former glory, seemed distant and uncertain. It was like witnessing a fading masterwork, slowly crumbling into obscurity.

The disappointment I felt was akin to watching a majestic painting stripped of its vibrant hues, or a symphony silenced before reaching its crescendo. My heartache was like a shattered sculpture, its fragments scattered across the barren ground, lost to the indifference of time.

I wondered if my Labor of love would be forever forgotten, buried under the weight of bureaucracy and the apathy of those who held the power to breathe life back into this forgotten marvel. The road, once a symbol of my pride, now stood as a painful reminder of dashed hopes and unfulfilled promises.

As I turned away from the road, my footsteps heavy with resignation, I couldn't help but feel a pang of melancholy. The memories of its splendour lingered in my mind, like whispers of a fading dream. I could only hope that one day, someone would see the potential that still lay dormant within its worn surface and give it the care and attention it so desperately needed.

For now, though, all I could do was carry the weight of disappointment in my heart, a burden borne by the architect who watched his creation crumble, and wonder if the road I built would ever find its way back to the realm of glory where it truly belonged

As I gazed upon the road, once my source of pride, I couldn't help but feel like a parent watching their child drift away, forgotten and abandoned. The road had become a reflection of my own longing, a silent plea for recognition, for the restoration of its former brilliance.

With a heavy heart, I knew that the fate of the road lay in the hands of those with the power to breathe life back into its worn veins. I hoped they would see beyond the cracks and potholes, beyond the faded paint and crumbling edges, and recognize the potential that lay dormant, yearning for revival.

For now, I could only stand there though invisible to humanity, a custodian of fading dreams, praying that the road I built, my chef-d'oeuvre, would find its way back to the realm of splendidness where it truly belonged.

The Amazing Christmas Gift

The air of Kadamsana Township buzzed with anticipation as Christmas Day dawned. It was a time for celebration, for exchanging gifts, for indulging in joyous celebrations. The true meaning of the day, the birth of Jesus Christ, seemed to have been overshadowed by a whirlwind of festivities. The community had transformed this sacred occasion into a personal extravaganza, a day to indulge in the desires of their hearts. Everyone was engulfed in the delight which the Christmas day brought to them. Contrary to expectations, it was a day when the worst sins were committed.

I had a friend whose feet never stepped on the floor of the church. Early in the morning of Christmas day, for the sake of nourishing his yearnings, he would rush to the market and buy a bottle of fruit juice, one kilogram of meat and two kilograms of rice which he would send to his wife by a bicycle taxi. Convinced that both his wife and child were well fed and safe, he would scamper straight, wave at the nuns at Salubeni Catholic Church, to Ma Phulani for a gourd of *masese,* the locally brewed beer. After that, he would trot to bottle stores and get 'cold' ones till mid-night. At exactly 00.01 hours, he would stagger home with a comprehensive feeling that the day had been well spent, though shouldering loads and loads of curses from his girlfriend, one of Ma Phulani's daughter, for not spending a night at her house.

For me and my family, we have always wanted to celebrate the day in a style befitting its Christmas purpose. Like spending the whole day worshipping and praising the Almighty mainly for the gift of life. Unfortunately, opposing strong forces from friends, neighbours and relatives had been propelling me to go eating and drinking without thinking 'too' much about God and Jesus. These friends changed my Christian expectations of Christmas. Unconsciously, I followed the majority, almost everybody, on Christmas day, spending my income and forgetting about life after Christmas, especially the month of January. I crowned the month of January, a high-ranking accolade of a general and called it 'General January'' because most people braved it with steeplechases; biting into the whole thirty plus one days without money.

On this material day, Chrissy, my long-time wife and friend, had prepared for this day long before and saved enough to pull down the 'General'. She calculated to spend the day indoors. Decorating the sitting room with a Christmas tree, beautiful flowers and a myriad of tiny fairy lights, she ensured that our radio was blaring out Christmas carols. Her expectation was that we would have visitors, but limited to sister-in law Nyakhave with her husband, Uncle Chrispin with his wife, Nephew Neffie, Brother Chipi and Bigman Chifundo. Their children were also invited. All of them would arrive around ten o'clock on foot, carrying their gifts. I imagined their faces breaking into laughter and smiles.

As we waited for them, a girl known as Aufi, about ten years old, slithered into our house. She was a Muslim girl who I thought had befriended Chrissy for a long time. I thought Chrissy had deliberately chosen not to tell me about her because of her shabby dress. All I thanked God for was that she was one of our visitors on this important day. Composed, she seemed to exactly know why she was here. We warmly welcomed her.

Earlier that day, Chrissy had confided in me that I had to give her enough money to buy all nice 'Christmas' things because we were likely to have visitors; some of whom we did not know. She was correct as it turned out to be.

Stuffed with brown chicken pieces, well cooked rice and a lot of vegetables, the dining table provoked my hunger to eat more than I always did. There was a five-litre bottle of fruit juice and a bottle of wine which Bigman Chifundo requested. As soon as they arrived, we ate, drank and made awful speeches, imitating our political leaders. Laughter, thanksgiving, dances and sounds of happy birthday songs mixed with shrieks of joy filled the air.

Aufi did not find pleasure in all this merry making. She stood aloof and leaned on the wall. Chrissy followed her, held her by the right shoulder. "Why so quiet? Let's go eat and drink. Feel free." Chrissy assured her.

Aufi, her face downcast, shrugged Chrissy off her shoulders. It was as if she was uncomfortable because of the bash that was unfamiliar to her.

"I saw you brought a black jumbo. Was that our gift? Where is it?" Chrissy, almost kneeling down to match her height, whispered.

"I hid it behind the house. I thought you would not accept such gifts as makaka (dry cassava) and nandolo (peas). I was about to throw them away."

"No. Please don't throw them away. Bring them here. In fact, my husband Richard likes them."

74

Aufi slipped out the back door, the weight of the world seemingly contained within the thoughts she clutched in her mind. Returning, she unburdened herself not on the floor, but on my wife's heart. First, she spilled the bitter truth of her mother's demise, a raw wound that hadn't healed since she saw her being interred. Then, she recounted the chilling death of one of her neighbours: a man who had been her pillar, a man of promise, and the gentle headmaster who had offered her a lifeline. "These tragedies," she lamented, "have cast a long, mournful shadow, erasing hope from my future. But I still have hope to meet Richard, your husband. It's my mother's wish that your husband should meet me and read the letter that she wrote two days before her death."

Chrissy's sympathy for her was palpable, and without hesitation, she invited me to the meeting. I gestured for Aufi to follow me as we made our way to a shaded spot beneath a sprawling mango tree. There, she began her story, starting with a heartfelt introduction to her mother—a remarkable woman known for her kindness and intelligence. As Aufi spoke, a glowing memory surfaced: I recalled the mother. She had been a beacon of achievement among her peers, excelling in her studies and graduating with good grades from senior secondary school. Yet despite her remarkable academic success and the pride she brought to her family, she faced an unexpected setback. Her path, once so promising, seemed obscured as she became pregnant and embraced the prospect of marriage, with her future now shrouded in uncertainty despite all her hard work.

I looked around to check if Chrissy was listening to this. I saw her laughing with nephew Neffie, a few metres away. Maybe she was jealous. Maybe she simply wanted to give me space. I failed to figure it out. I simply turned to check Aufi's face. She was bathed in tears. Ten minutes later, she handed me the black jumbo with a letter in a torn envelope.

"Before my mother died, she advised me that I must give you this parcel on Christmas day." Aufi said.

"Thank you." I immediately threw it into my trouser pocket. "I will read it later. Let's go back into the house." I told the girl.

Straight from the place, I rushed to where Chrissy stood and opened the letter. It read:

Dear Richard,

I hope you will understand what I want to say. First of all, I would like to ask for your forgiveness. You must forgive me because I have opted to write to you after a long time and wish you to read this after my death. For many years, I have lived on earth as a very bitter woman. I never achieved what I wanted in life. I was double fooled. Firstly, I trusted my parents more than I did to myself. I never focused on the bright future which my teachers thought I had. Secondly, I would like you to forgive me for denying to accept you after I carried your pregnancy. You said you were willing to take me as your wife and 'see the baby grow healthy and attain good education as you did. For several times, you tried to convince me; but I was adamant, not from deep down my heart. I listened to my mother who said you were not rich so I should not be tied to a beggar. I had to marry a fisherman who already had two wives, that much you know, just because he was rich. I feel sorry to have let you down. Thirdly, it was painful to abandon my Christianity for Islam to satisfy the wishes of my husband. When your child was born, she

76

was named Aufi by a man who was not her father. Four years later, as you are aware, the man died. Five years after he died, I tried to make ends meet on my own but I could not succeed. When I fell sick, I sent you a message to come and see me but, for obvious reasons, you did not. That time, even now, there is a lot of pain all over my body. My words are few. Richard, please forgive me. I had to write this letter because the future of Aufi is uncertain. Accept her as my Christmas gift to you.

Sincerely,

Martha.

Dusk had fallen. Chrissy was willing to see my reaction. She must have observed that I had been nervous. While the guests in their drunken state were chatting loudly, she leaned on the wall as she waited for my explanation. Aufi was still inside the house, staring at the guests. My mind was full of doubts. What would be her reaction to this? I begged her to follow me out into the evening air. The sky was bright with stars but my heart was dark, laden with the weight of this unforeseen circumstance. When we reached where the light from the security bulb was glowing ridiculously, I threw the letter on her palms. She looked at me, read it silently and heaved out a sigh.

"Let's go inside. Aufi is a special gift for us on Christmas day. A gift from God."

I nodded my head, in affirmation.

As the guests were staggering back home, Chrissy prepared a bed for Aufi. I wouldn't think she was right, for I least expected such a welcoming reaction, but I acknowledged that she knew what she was doing.

Dear Newborn

Dear newborn.

I like the way you massage my face with your little hand. Do not be afraid. Go on as I cradle you in my arms, and my timid voice rises in a gentle melody. The melody that goes, …

Da!kaziyenda

Da!ayenda mawa

Da!kaziyenda

Da!ayenda mawa.

This lullaby, sung in Chichewa, the language of my people, is a plea for you to walk towards me. It is a song we've sung to other children for generations, a reminder of our journey and the challenges we've faced. Yet, even as we sing it to each other, we find ourselves still struggling to walk. Now, as the newest member of our family, I sing it to you, hoping that you might find the strength to walk a path that we have yet to fully understand.

The village we are in is called Gumbi. Gumbi is a myriad story and a soundless song. Every time I try to put words on a paper about

78

this village, bad memories come to life. I do not deliver what I intend to. I have done that before, turning and turning around a point. Issues are many. I introduce a topic and then leave it, introduce another one until I am told to let it go because I have no point.

This is Gumbi. Our haven. Our country. Be happy and laugh, but not so loud. Your mother was born here. Her forefathers plowed this soil before the same soil ate them. They were buried under it. Their forefathers fought for this land. They fought all wars. The John Chilembwe war. The independence war. The referendum war. The Madandu war. They won the land, but not the freedom.

You will meet Uncle Ted and his likes, who hide the truth from young people. Always involved in shady business. Uncle Ted, cannot tell you what he did to accumulate all the wealth he has or why he keeps his arrogant wife whose womb is as hard as a stone. He is always quiet. If you ask for any assistance, he will keep his mouth shut or say, *'ndilibe'* (I do not have one). He is just as good as those gone before us. Let him live in his own society, the society of hiding to tell the truth that may also benefit others. A Brainless buffoon…

Now, here we are. When you stand on an anthill over there, overlooking Mpombedza hills in the west and throw your eyes deep into the neighbourhood, you will see a boundary of life. I call it the boundary of life because you will never get what you want without bumping into a wall. There is a thick wall there. Once you get close, you will see midgets moving in circular paths punctuated by naked hills, dry rivers, grass-thatched huts, dusty roads, dilapidated school blocks, malnourished children clinging on the back of their skinny mothers. Loan sharks confronting poorly dressed civil servants. And no yields in the fields. Such is our life. We don't like it though we are failing to say it out loud.

Look up, they say the sky's the limit. Listen to them, but do not trust them. We know our limits. We know where our pursuit of education will stop. We know what jobs are at stake for us. We know what type of pills we will swallow and we know when we will die. That is our situation here. You can't go beyond that. There is a gate, a gate of life and a huge 'lock' on it says; "This is not for you." They created those 'locks' for us because we are black.

We live like this, and we accepted it. I am your father. She is your mother, and over there is your grandmother. She likes children. She loves cleaning dirty children, most of the time without soap. And she doesn't bother to ask for anything to beautify her skin. She is patiently waiting for her death. She will carry you one day. I found her like this, and we enjoy seeing her like this. We laugh with her. She taught us to laugh even when we are in problems, and we love it. We lost Apiye, your mother's father, a long time ago. He taught us to be ourselves. We accepted what he told us. He said we must not ask for more than a daily bread. And here we are, hopping from grass to grass.

I did not grow up here. My home village is in the Shire Valley. I personally do not like the place. It is hot, very hot. Ever since I left the place, I have never thought of visiting my people. And my people have never wished to visit me. I do not believe they have an idea that I am alive. Maybe, they think, I died a long time ago or I am still in prison. People would hate you if you were once imprisoned. They fear you. They run away from you. They do not wish to give you any opportunity. They chase you. You are locked, but from outside. You need keys to unlock the relationship, love and care. But even if you do, they will not accept you. Trust is an important asset. Once lost, you cannot reclaim it. My people locked me out. Nobody visits me and wishes to give me a second chance. I wanted to live like others and pursue careers that will turn around my situation. When I tried to raise my voice against violation of human rights, only a few people understood, but they were voiceless. I was bundled into a police van and thrown into prison. When you are poor your voice is hardly heard

New born, your arrival is a blessing. Being the only male in the house, I have waited for so long as to tell you how life is lived in this village. I would not tell any boy. I wanted to tell my own boy. Even though your eyes are not ripe enough to see petals of the world and tips of thorns that prick our minds every day, I would love to tell you before your tongue is scorched with pepper that those who matter hide behind their 'painted' faces. Scrawny, my eyes are tired and soon they will begin to see men like trees. My handwriting is gradually becoming illegible and soon my memory will be watered down. Death is at the door. Only 'Him' knows my destiny. I have never seen a leader permanently helping the poor people. I know of beer parties and their colours.

Gumbi is not transforming and—at the pace it is tackling development issues—will take ages to transform. Every five years 'pregnant' men come. It's my wish that you shouldn't meet them in your lifetime. They give hope as they talk about building good schools, hospitals, bridges and roads. But hardly are these promises fulfilled.

Dear newborn, my days are numbered. Many of the strong structures that have welcomed you, existed during the time of your great-grandmother. There are leaders across the world. We hear about them on radios and televisions: most of them, especially leaders who wear our skin, maul resources they find in a country. We had resources here. Trees in Chikanga forest, Uranium in Kayere, land, as well as intelligent people. You can't find them. They were taken away.

Dear newborn. Take this letter as a fatherly gift describing life in Gumbi, our home. Be ambitious. Do not rely on people. Work hard and the treasure I have for you is in the form of the words you are hearing now. Luck will be on your side so long you carry my words with you. Hard work pays. Don't say my father failed me. I was not all that lucky. I did not see a silver spoon in my mouth. I beg you to grow up strong and strive for the best in your life.

I am your father, no doubt about it. I will leave my name with you. Be free to use it anywhere, and in any way, you want it. Be free to visit my village, and introduce yourself without fear. If people will not recognize you, do something good that they should recognize you. People will be happy to stay with you or to keep you if you do something that identifies you. Be free to say whatever you want to say, but do not harm people.

I would love it if you visit my relatives. They are charming people, and they live in the Shireni Valley. You will not struggle to trace them because they are among the elite in the society. They carry the banner of the group village head, and they are the most respected. Respect is part of our culture. I know with time this aspect will diminish looking at how multiculturalism is sweeping away the indigenous cultures, but I would advise you to respect people just as they wish to be respected. You will lose nothing. One thing that will be paramount is that everybody will say nothing but good things about you. Our people love to be respected. However, be aware that people love easy life, but as for you, work hard, be independent. You may not be received by my people because you are a son of a prisoner, but still plan to visit them.

Before I hand you over to your mother, let me tell you about Paul, your brother. Some people will be brave to tell you about him, but they will not tell you the way I want it. This is the first story I think I must share with you. I used to be a brave man but I sold it on the death of Paul. A brave man does not cry, but surely, I had to. Not in a day but months. Paul was a young brave boy just like yourself. Always quiet. Always eager to tamper with my pocket radio. At three, he was enjoying himself when I played music on my cassette player, but most importantly, he would be very excited if he did it by himself. He wouldn't throw the radio on the ground as her mother would think, but fiddle with it very carefully until some music is played. A future engineer or a future disc-jockey he was. Quickly, he learnt how to pronounce 'dad' and quickly he was able to differentiate relatives from family friends. I liked him so much because his face was as unapologetic as mine.

I wouldn't think too much about Paul's death and be quick to blame witches and wizards to agree with your mother, but I blamed public hospitals. At that time there were no drugs in the hospitals. Every sick person was going to Mapwelemwe, the witchdoctor, to hear who was bewitching them, and have their bodies cut and smeared with black oily substances. I wouldn't go there with Paul. I knew herbs could cure malaria, but witchdoctors had a tendency of teaching witchcraft to children so that they would have a lot of clients in future. Paul suffered from malaria. Your mother scampered to this clinic but to no avail. I jogged to mission clinics to meet colleagues—nurses, Medical Assistants and Health Surveillance Assistants—whom I thought would help but it yielded nothing. Remember, I am a graduated prisoner.

Poverty is a disease that can be cured by strong determination. If you do not have prominent people around you, people who understand modern tricks—people with a kind heart—you will not come out of it. You can go to school, attain the very necessary credentials but if you are poor your opinion will not be respected. Famous people around you will not acknowledge that you can reasonably assist them. Born a *takataka* and a nonentity, you will die a *takataka* and a nonentity. That's our theory. The same trickles down to your children and your grandchildren. That's a poverty cycle. If you want to break it, work hard.

I did not talk when clinicians wrote the prescription in Paul's health passport book without giving me the drugs. I wouldn't think this was unprofessional to prescribe drugs which they would not administer. I wouldn't believe that there were no drugs when each and every day these clinics were opened. Why wouldn't they close and march in the streets? Wasn't this a serious matter? Turning to look at the door of the clinic, and the clinician who was waving at me, I wouldn't believe in everything they said. I thought and still think that drugs are meant for the popular people, for they were driving into these clinics and coming out happier than before while Paul, your brother, was rolling and crying in pain, begging for life. I must not hide this to you. If you will, dear newborn, grow up and become a doctor, you must learn to love all people. Sick people need timely care. We lost Paul because of lack of love and negligence.

Be aware that life is full of eventualities. Your mother had no money and therefore failed to take Paul to private hospitals. Uncle Ted had and has money, but his wife is a 'sick' lady. Her leprosy is too hard to allow her hand to dip into her pocket. Her mouth is the worst; she would speak anything from nonsense to absurd. She doesn't care about family relationships. I feared approaching them. Your mother dared not. Paul died when there was somebody we could talk to. We were afraid, yet they came in their cars and mourned Paul. After consoling us, they went away. We remained and continued to live like this.

Before I conclude, let me tell you that your mother forgot something very important. And it was that which was forgotten that led to Paul's demise. It is not good to forget. People get into trouble because of forgetting. It is not negligence, but they just forget. Nobody thinks it is a non-communicable disease. People do forget at a time when you do not think they can forget. They even confess, swear in the name of the lord, and suggest you cut their fingers, persuading you to think they can't forget. It is just very unfortunate. A lot of people are in trouble because of forgetting. And it is bad when people forget to tell the truth. Your mother forgot that Paul did not swallow any malaria drug. When the clinician, your mother met, suggested that Paul should not take any other malaria drug assuming he had taken 'fansidar' a few weeks before as per the prescription in Paul's health passport book, she simply walked away, unknowingly to bewail the passing of Paul. In the evening, she prayed for Paul. The young boy looked at her with great expectation; his eyes turning to his God to give her the right direction. The more she prayed, the more his head throbbed. He wished he had stopped her, and forced her to take him back to hospital. Young as he was, Paul died without protest, without a Parthian shot.

Such is our life. We live in suffering and death. We only have hope about life after death. Your mother developed hypertension a few years ago. She is in trouble. Your grandmother coughs a lot. We do not know what it is. Each and every day, we pick up our frail bodies to the garden and back. We have nothing to do. We have ourselves to present our grievances to. When you are grown up into a man, learn to present your grievances to yourself. Nobody will lift you up from your mud if you don't work hard. Let's go back.

Mashongo

Mashongo took his life. As a Parthian shot, he wrote; "…Thabongo doesn't think I am a human being. Taking workers as cogs in a machine, he looks at us like objects. …I am his object. He hates me too much, that much you know. Let him live. I cannot afford to be in the company of people who do not like me. I am a social being. I cannot be sad all the days of my life…. Tell Sheila, we will meet in heaven."

That morning, I woke up with a gluttonous thirst to hunt for Mashongo and meet him alive, against the harsh intolerable wind that he had died. First to search was in Sheila's house. It was impossible that Sheila wouldn't know where Mashongo had gone or what had happened to him. On two occasions, Sheila unzipped Mashongo's trousers and sucked it when they met at the toilets behind Villa Tourist Club while I was with them.   And when loan sharks threatened to confront and nearly strip him naked, it was Sheila who hid him in her house.

Surely, Mashongo was Sheila's somebody, though both of them used to deny before us. I nearly believed them until Sheila, after getting tired of hiding him and cooking false information, decided to bite my ear that Mashongo's next cave of hiding was her house. They would have been good lovers for all workers at Mandalena factory smelled a rotten fish, and they were always teasing him about her. But Mashongo would simply laugh it off.

To Sheila's house I had to go because Mashongo might have been hiding there, not that he was dead. It was obvious that something was wrong with Mashongo but nobody would explain better than Sheila. Since there was nothing—a kind of an enlightenment—coming from Sheila's mouth, I faulted the sincerity of what I heard. Sheila, knowing that I was Mashongo's friend and was solving his problems with a sense of maturity, would have apprised me of his state of mind before his death.

The whole factory was inundated with the wind that Mashongo was no more, and his body was at Lilongwe City Morgue, 280 kilometres away.

I took a half cup of tea with a slice of bread, brushed my teeth and darted towards the door. A striking light like a flash of a camera shot through the window and painted a zero on the wall. I closed all the windows and made sure that all the curtains were drawn. I left the house. If it really was true that Mashongo had kissed the dust, I was ready not to come back until his body was buried. I was about to jump the last steps on the veranda when the door clicked back into the lock. I returned to remove the keys. I wouldn't hide my emotions but sang to myself, 'Mashongo, why? Mashongo, why?'

It was normal for confused workers like Mashongo to abandon the job soon after pay, and come back when their pockets were unoccupied. It was also not a surprise to see loan sharks hovering around the premises to ask for muddled workers like Mashongo who were always defaulting payments. And it was common to see kaunjika sellers being cheated. Not forgetting those who sold thobwa, the sweet brew. Such was life at the factory. Mashongo was not spared from this bondage. For the past four months, he had been borrowing money from me in order for him to settle some of his debts. Such was his life. Always requesting for small loans. Five days before, he did not come to see me soon after pay. He just disappeared. Because he did not give me back my money, I was sure he was just roving like a lost cow in the thickets of fear, and chose not to report for duties. It then would make sense to check him at Sheila's house rather than believe that he was dead. I wouldn't trust the messenger. The messenger was known for telling lies. He was a bit careless with his mouth.

I knew Mashongo, he was somehow angry but hang himself he would not. He was old and reasonable enough to differentiate right from wrong. He would tell the effects of every narcotic drug he sniffed, evidence that he knew what he was doing. He was not a fraidy-cat that he could end his life with a rope. As an alcoholic, he had many friends including Sheila who could comfort him. So, I had to look for Sheila to endorse my doubts.

I came to know Sheila when she was sharing a cigarette with Mashongo at Villa Tourist Club, and immediately sensed that I had met a cunning 'actor.' She beckoned me while shaking her bottom to hook me in. A puff of smoke fled out of her nostrils, covered the whole of her face and disappeared into the sky. I looked away but stood there to listen to her. I knew her message was abstract. When Sheila raised her eyebrows and greeted me again, I immediately brushed off my fear that she could be a claimed property. And when she almost knelt down to scratch my palm, my guess was right. Sheila was an expert at catching strangers into her net, and sucked their dick for the serpent's soup. And, despite her presence in the bar and carefree lifestyle, I wouldn't think she was not responsible. Some ladies like Sheila would be responsible— being school teachers, nurses, police officers— but patronize in beer places like everybody else, serve any willing patron and accommodate them in their homes. They would want to live like others, but somewhere along the way they might have missed the 'bongo' of marriage.

Mashongo wouldn't end his life like a fool. He was not one.

Thabongo, the Human Resources Manager, called me to his office.

"We have lost the drug addict. May his soul rest in peace," he said. I kept quiet. "At least you have heard what has happened." He continued. I confessed dishonestly that I had heard nothing.

"You see, the Directors have been warning him, but he was just a nincompoop. His drug addiction has killed him."

"Sorry for what you are telling me, boss. I must request that you give me enough time to look for him. He is my friend. I know he might be hiding somewhere. He is not dead. I don't trust the gardener's mouth. Did you go to the City Mortuary yourself?"

"That's the reason I called for you. Go to the City Mortuary. Verify the news."

Around ten o'clock, I called Sheila. We agreed to meet at the Club.

Mashongo was deceptively a good man, always quiet when he was not drunk and had a good choice of words when speaking. Only his way of thinking was debatable. He was quick to anger. The moment I noticed this; I made up my mind that I had to try my level best to change this attitude of his. I thought I knew his problem. He was a victim of depression. I had to help him get away with it. Put him side by side with Thabongo, Mashongo was the most intelligent and educated person, but was not promoted. That could be the source of his ineffectuality. He was two years ahead of me in college and got his degree with a distinction. When I joined him in the department, I felt sorry to see that he had stooped so low as not to be trusted. With his new friend—the 'big' cigarette—slowly, he had become an abnormal person but no one would wish to have him fired. I personally wouldn't allow myself to see him like that. I wouldn't want to see him running in the streets next time. I wouldn't like it if I saw him carrying a bag of filth and helping himself from dust bins. I wouldn't want to lose him. Further, I wouldn't want to believe my uncle's theory that all intelligent people are mad, and all mad people are intelligent so that I could justify why Mashongo had to be mad. Who would run the affairs of this country if all intelligent people were confined in a mental hospital?

At the door of the Club, I met Sheila. She was lighting a cigarette.

"Thanks, Max. You are here on time." She grinned.

"This is Friday, Men's Day." I added.

"Let me burn this cigar behind the building. I will join you shortly in order to chat comfortably."

91

I turned to look at her short pink dress. It was spectacular especially that I was able to see her through. Seen from afar, both her underwear and bra were white. Glistening around her waist, beads of different colours were neatly packed. It was as if she had just taken a shower because the perfume, she was wearing was just good. To match with her dress, the earrings dangling below her short hair were also amazing. Her hairy sexy plump legs took her round the building. It was right to suggest that she was appetizingly prepared to clean the 'guns' of men and aid them carefully to shoot on target.

"You seem to like her today."

That was the voice of a bar man whose name was Gwati. I ignored his statement by ordering my favourite drink.

I wouldn't sit on a tall stool and listen to Gwati's comments about the ongoing premiership league. So, I strolled out and sat on a plastic chair outside the bar to reflect on my assignment. The sun was just a quarter away before noon. I was not in a hurry anyway to ask everybody about Mashongo fearing that I would raise an alarm. I waited for somebody to ask me about who had died at our workplace. I thought, by now, the story would have been dancing on people's lips.

Gwati—the man I knew very long ago because we once worked together at First Revenue Administration—pulled his chair and joined me to engage me in the premiership league debate. Shuddering, he was holding an extra-large bottle of his favourite drink. Just after a few sips, he asked me about Mashongo. I jokingly told him that I was not Mashongo's keeper. I was supposed to protect the identity of my colleague. Gwati, as if he knew something, pestered me with a lot of questions that I replied cunningly until Sheila pulled her chair and sat very close to me.

"Max, ndilibe mowa (Max, I have no beer)." She smiled.

"Talk to Gwati. I will foot that bill."

As she rose to enter the bar to pick a bottle by herself, Gwati talked about the lady's parasitism. I agreed with him, though he might have forgotten that in our culture prostitutes do not foot their own bills. They are flowers. Such flowers can make bad days good, sometimes. If one would walk into the Club and find no woman, they gave a lot of excuses like "today, I just want to pass time. I am in no drinking mood" as opposed to "barman, dress the table" when two or three women were brandishing their make-up, and speaking lovelier than their wives.

The minute Sheila took two long sips, I grabbed her arm and pulled her aside.

"I trust you because you trust me." I said.

"Really?"

"Yes. This I have said in case you didn't know."

"I must be a happy person if this is really coming from the bottom of your heart."

"Forget about what you are thinking. I am looking for Mashongo. Please help me find him." I whispered.

"Is he not reporting for duties again?"

She moved her eyes across the place, and the thud of her flat shoes whispered on the floor.

"Wait. Please come back."

"Let me ask the barman."

"No, Wait. Let's finish the beer first."

We went back to the place. Gwati was nosey. He asked whether the impromptu meeting was about Mashongo or my desire to have a 'short time' sex with Sheila in a room behind the place. Sheila jumped in and said, "It's none of your business."

Mashongo was not renting a house like all other workers were but one of the rooms behind Izoizo bar. There was an agreement between the bar owner and Mashongo that he be an acting bar manager, assisting in making sure that the place looked tidy and reporting any shortage that the bar man incurred after knocking off from the factory. How he liked the job I wondered, but a graduate of the most prominent university and a qualified engineer, Mashongo would not turn into a bartender. This was what attracted me to ensure that this colleague of mine was freed from such a servitude. However, out of his two jobs, he would not manage a proper home but a room which was meant for a prostitute. Unlucky for him—any prostitute who was hired to extinguish fire from his trousers—went away with either a blanket or mattress for failing to honour his 'payment' commitment. At the time I bumped into him, Mashongo had only a toothbrush and a bunch of clothes to point as his wealth. Surely, something must have been wrong with him, but he wouldn't reach an extent of begging in the streets while I watched. After sharing some jokes, I reminded Sheila that time was rife to start the search. She invited another lady so that we would be three. She said we should begin from his place. As we passed by a place where local beer was sold, I did not believe the drama before my eyes. I just thought Sheila was playing a game I did not know. As usual, she begged some money to buy a cigarette while she was trying to find information about our target. When I stood alone, I whispered to myself; 'Mashongo. Why, Mashongo?

Through the lens of Thabongo, I happened to know the other side of Mashongo towards work the time he was introducing me to all members of staff office by office. Almost forty years old, short and fat, Thabongo was very smart to propel the boats of regionalism, nepotism and tribalism. Hating workers of other tribes such as Mashongo was his duty of care above discussing production and sales performance of the factory. He told me how bad Mashongo was, how he thought Mashongo had betrayed the factory owners, where Mashongo had failed and the very fact that I was hired to replace Mashongo. "He is intelligent but we cannot keep him." That statement did not fly out of my mind. He was not loved not because he was a non-performer, but natural hatred. Some workers like Mashongo wouldn't be liked by others when their qualification supersedes others, when they come from a particular tribe, and when they upgrade themselves. The tribal thinking might have degraded the worker's unity, but stupid minds like Thabongo's would always think of tribes instead of embracing workers for their capabilities.

Sheila came back.

Walking in a hurry, ahead of us, she jumped into Izoizo bar and went straight to the bar man. I thought that strategy would not work but she knew what she was doing. I stood outside and chose to hide behind the hedge. She brought two bottles of beer; one for me and another for herself on my bill.

"Max, wait here. I will find you," she said.

I followed her with my eyes as she pushed a small door that led to where Mashongo slept. I heaved a sigh when a thought came to my mind. It was a negative one. What if he was not there?

It did not take long. Sheila rushed into the bar again. She lit a cigarette and strolled towards me to announce that Mashongo left four days before, and he was nowhere to be seen. Mashongo, why Mashongo?

Go to the City Morgue therefore we had to. Sheila nodded.

I knew Mashongo as a straight-forward character. I got to know this during one of the first management meetings we invited him to attend. Slender but with a baritone voice, as he was being disparaged, he made his eyes pop in and out cantankerously. This he demonstrated when, considered as a good example of a slothful worker, he was being crucified on the cross of embarrassment or stripped naked in order to amplify the reasons for being a possible candidate for dismissal. He had been quiet when Thabongo was cooking up stories against him. Everybody in the meeting room heard that he was indolent, good for nothing and had to go. Dr Slong, the Managing Director, adjusted her pair of sunglasses before she asked whether Mashongo was listening to what Thabongo was saying or not. Instead, a sudden thought crossed his mind. He stood up, pushed his table hard and sat down. Turning his head to look at everybody in the room, he saw Dr Slong's eyes begging him to sit down. She might have read his mind that he was up to pounce on his enemy. He felt it was unprofessional for everybody at the factory to know that he was to be dismissed in a meeting like that. And, it was also not important to announce who was to replace him. Mashongo felt that both Thabongo and Dr. Slong were stupid. Just the two of them, behind closed doors, were enough to tell him the fate of his job. The whole factory would get the wind of it through an internal memo. Simple management logic.

Before he defiantly walked out of the room, he pointed his index finger at Thabongo.

"If you call yourself, Human Resources Manager, you must be a stupid one. Son of a dog!"

Since then, he had been waiting for his letter of dismissal—which was yet to come while executing his duties opposite my desk– until the time I was commissioned to seek the truth of his death. So, it was indeed impractical, torture, cruelty, insensitivity and tactlessness to warn a person that his position had been filled without having both his face and name deleted in the books of the factory. Shame on Thabongo!

Seated at the back of a cab, heading to the City Morgue, Sheila and I joined three other people including the driver who were engrossed with listening to unofficial results of the parliamentary and presidential elections. My right hand resting on her left thigh, Sheila aided me to insert my hand deeper, between her legs, so that my fingers could reach her most sophisticated part. She stretched them wide and open. Immediately, the gun in my trousers started unfolding itself. Sheila noticed and responded by putting her left hand over my shoulders so that her fingers were toying with my left ear at her will. Attempting to kiss me, she planted her lips on my right cheek but I avoided her because of a cigarette smell that her mouth was emitting. Though I had a desire to taste her, I believed I would be sucking the serpent's soup.

"Feel free." She disturbed my thoughts.

"Action is speaking loudly." I nodded.

We talked on a number of issues but Sheila couldn't tell me her age, the number of children she had, the number of years she had been in her profession and the number of men who had tasted her. She only talked about her beauty, not even the number of scars on her body which she hid in make-up nor mental scars and what brought them. She was astute. Before I asked her anything negative, she already had a better explanation for it. I asked several questions, but the reply was 'Just do what you want. The ball is in your hands. And this is your time. Use it accordingly.' Given such a mandate, I became more flexible, and looked forward to doing the sucking once we reached Lilongwe City.

The car cruised on the winding road, slicing through fog, and headed towards the city. It went round two hills following a truck that was making for Lizulu market a few kilometres before our destination. Two of the passengers had instructed the driver not to overtake it because it was carrying their baskets of tomatoes and other commodities to sell so they were to check if the drivers did not steal. It would have been boring to be driven slowly, but the market was not too far. It was cold in the month of June following the heavy rain that fell during the planting season.

When I noticed that the driver of the cab was slender and had a baritone voice, Mashongo's face zoomed in my mind. Just like Mashongo, the driver liked commenting about politics. He was a staunch supporter of one of the political parties such that you wouldn't tell him to change his mind. If he were in the cab, he would convince all the people that his party would win the elections. You would believe him if you wanted to cut the long story short though most of his facts were without foundation. The only thing I would live to remember about him was that he wouldn't become angry if he met an opponent who would swear to engage him into debate until sunset. In most cases, he would brag about his party, its leader, and if his opponent had more facts than him, he would conclude the debate by saying 'we are brothers and sisters of the same mother Malawi. Just buy me a bottle of beer and a cigarette. Life goes...' Laughter would be ignited in Sheila and I for that was what Mashongo would be up to. His arguments were just a bait for camaraderie. We called him a chatterbox in a silent shadow.

The cab took us straight to the City Lodge. I had to eat her pussy before we entered into a mourning mood. As soon as she closed the door of the room we booked, she unzipped my trousers and started sucking it. I waved to her to stop it for my gun was about to shoot sperms into her mouth. While my middle-left finger was in her vagina, and as hot as it was, I started firing on the ground. She quickly jumped onto the bed and lay flat and invited me to pour the serpent's soup into her vagina. Both of us were too hot to talk about a

99

condom. I ate her pussy four times before we left the room to the City Police.

The Police informed us that a man identified as Mashongo had indeed killed himself in one of the rooms at the City Lodge, according to the scanty information in the visitor's book. One of the police officers interrogated us at length about why we thought the man who had died was our relative. We were quick to add that our relative was slim, had a goatee, and smoked a lot. Sheila added that he had a large scar on his right thigh. At that point, the police officer's face brightened. He flushed out a letter that was found on the bed where Mashongo was found dead. We displayed it on the floor.

Dear Max,

I wouldn't die without biting your ear a little. You must have heard that I am dead. That is true. I am dead, not because I am a chicken or that I am afraid of surviving harsh conditions, but I want to give others a chance. Especially you. I know you have been uncomfortable to execute your duties well because of me. You were told you had to replace me but until now, I was not fired. I have decided to terminate my contract in this way. Max, feel free. Set your own standards.

As a human being I wouldn't think that I was wallowing in an accepted curse. At school, my friends didn't work as much as I did. They enjoyed life at school. They are still enjoying life after school. My case is what you already know. Apart from drinking and smoking, I have never had a chance of enjoying life in a different way. I didn't sleep many nights to perfect my assignment at the expense of social life. I left college without a fiancée because I wanted a distinction. Got it, I dreamed big. I cheated myself. 'My parents will drive my car, live in an electrified house of their own and be proud of me.' Unfortunately, they have waited for so long. That dream is not coming forth. They wrote to me that they are not at peace. It's a big disappointment to them after they toiled hard to educate me. My parents, all alive, are frail. They are still surviving though without my support. I have let them down big time. You may wish to talk to them at my funeral.

I cannot blame you in all this. I have worked with you, though for a stint. You are such an amazing man. I would laugh, smile, be with everybody but honestly, I was alone looking at objects instead of people. You have been encouraging and supporting me. You have done your part. However, you found me while I was already in a difficult situation. Through thick and thin, I have endured enough. You know what I mean. Thabongo doesn't think I am a human being. Taking workers as cogs in a machine, he looks at people like objects. In his eyes, I am his object. He hates me too much, you know. Let him live. I cannot afford to be in the company of people who do not like others. I am a social being. At some point I have to smile, laugh, but I cannot be sad all the days of my life. I am dead because I want Thabongo to live and rule comfortably.

You would say, like you always did, that life is dynamic. One day, my situation would improve. I have been trusting your piece of advice, but the weight of my problems was too big. Last year, I wanted to resign and join another organization. The way I know Thabongo things wouldn't work. People like Thabongo cannot be escaped.

They have stone hearts. They would follow you everywhere to prove that you are useless, and they do not think that, doing so, wounding a person for no wrongdoing is too painful. I am fed up with Thabongo, the beast, and anybody like him. I would move into another organization but I will still find a Thabongo of some sort. I have lived a life of self-deception for so long. Let me go. Let Thabongo live.

Sheila will not be happy with this news. Tell her I loved her and will love her forever. My spirit will always be with her. She is a nice lady, and must always be nice to people. She has my child. I kept this secret because that's what we agreed. Please tell her to reveal who among her three sons is mine. Take care of him. What I would have loved to see and hear is for her to quit that business and marry. She is a marriage material. I enjoyed her kisses.

When you finish reading this letter, arrange to have my body buried next to my brother who died when he was two. Tell my parents about this.

Lastly, tell Sheila, we will meet in heaven.

Mashongo.

The Nightmare

It was exactly 4.30 a.m. when an alarm buzzed. I woke up and peeped out of the window. Darkness had not completely left. The day was approaching like a crawling baby, slowly with patches of fog. The fog that had covered the factories in the industrial area was ridiculously rolling up in Ndirande hills and systematically disappearing into the sky.

In this tropical country, the fog was announcing the arrival of a clear sunny day. That morning Dora was calm. Her silence was quite unusual. As she prepared breakfast, she did not sing her most favourite song 'sewere, umlange mwana' (mother-in law, advise your girl) as she often used to. An air of quietness enveloped the house. She did not switch on the radio as she did on many other mornings. I sat on the bed and corked up my ears, but it was as if Dora was sick. All I heard was a series of coughs, not persistent though. I moved closer to her.

"Dora, are you ready for the journey?"

She did not reply.

"I am asking you. Are you taking me to see Namgabi, your mother?"

She chose to remain silent. Silence is golden, but in this context, silence is silvery. What it meant for me to be silent was a dislike of the journey. What else?

Surely, she was not willing to go; rather she was not interested in giving me an opportunity to see her parents. How could she do that after I had already promised her? I returned to the bedroom. No sooner had I sat on the bed than Dora sneaked in as tears snaked down her cheeks. Why these tears? I took a glance at her dress. It was wet. Something immediately came to my mind. Either I was not safe to travel with her or she was not safe to walk out of the compound.

This was in connection with what we watched on the TV the previous night. It was broadcast that some minorities were being killed, their body parts sold to neighbouring countries. The TV showed the dead bodies of the victims. I tried to connect that it might have been a source of stress for Dora. I moved closer to her and embraced her. She was seemingly in trouble but for the fact that she did not want me to help in decision-making I patiently awaited, perhaps she would come round. Some moments later, normal senses brightened her face but she did not reveal the watershed of her distress.

Towards half past six, we strolled towards the main bus depot in the city. Gestures were all we relied upon to be in touch so our communication was limited to a yes or no answer. Whatever it was, I was still happy to fulfill my promise. At least this action would be proof that I had no time to joke with her. I had already confided in her that once I made a decision, I stuck to it. She would marry me. That's what I wanted her to witness that day.

We were heading south; her home village was in the Southern Region. When the bus started off, she immediately turned her face to me. That was the time when my eyes were glued on a certain couple who were quarrelling in the bus about the impotency of the man.

"Look at me, Denis. Do you really love me?"

I said yes.

"Denis, are you sure?"

I said yes. "You know I declared it already, Dora."

"Look at me, Denis. Are you serious?"

I suggestively looked at her face long enough. She also did the same before she shyly looked away.

"Do your questions relate to our skin differences perhaps?" I asked.

The bus jerked. We were travelling to Mangunda, one of the remotest parts of that region. For me, this was an adventure that would make me believe whether my fiancée was not cheating on me or not. I forced her to take me to that place for I wanted to show a commitment to our relationship. I never saw anything that could give me a clue that I did not break her virginity. Her breasts were firm. In fact, I knew that there were some Chinese herbs which acted as breast firmer; but I was not an expert in those fields.

In this tropical country, a virgin is proved through the breasts. If a lady has big breasts that look like paw paws, most young unmarried men like me tend to question the virginity of the lady.

It was around noon when the bus halted at a place where we would find a path that would take us to see who happened to be Dora's relatives; the only surviving relatives, her mother. I also expected to see two children, a boy and a girl, who would welcome us hilariously. In fact, she told me that her sister passed away some two years before and had left a number of children who were staying with her mother at Mangunda. There were no shops at the place. A good number of bicycle taxis were taking their passengers to the opposite direction only. I wanted to drink water but the nearest borehole according to Dora was five kilometers away, which she doubted whether it was functioning or not. Half way the distance, Dora branched off to see a lady who was harvesting sweet potatoes. I did not hear what they were discussing but the lady pointed at a small hill that was behind another hill that looked like a tall tree among shorter ones as if she was giving directions. Of course, I am old enough to tell through gestures what probably would have been the matter. Dora had overstayed in the city. Did that mean she had forgotten her home, a place that had taught her the very essential things of life? A place where she spent most of her childhood and early education? That thought died in its infancy. I panicked but when love has mounted its camp, even jealous hearts cannot be destroyed.

Even true stories told to warn you about the dirtiest things that your fiancée had done before, even as close to time as yesterday, ignorance cures it all. I remained silent though I had a burning desire to ask. I wobbled down the road, up and down the hills until I saw a village when the sun was about to set. I pretended not to be tired but honestly, I was completely worn-out. The surroundings of the place were more like a deserted place than a dwelling place. The hut we were approaching was newly built. It was as if it was set up to welcome us. Dora did not indicate to me that we had reached our destination but insightful knowledge guided me to the realization that we had reached our destination. That was not without a clue. Dora offloaded the bag from the head and opted to carry it as if it was not heavy at all. Big question: Will my would-be apongozi be a sing'anga? This question directed at me confused the one who flung it. The hut looked like one of a witch doctor. A traditional song shrouded my mind and touched my heart,

'kapilire unka iweko/kapilire unka iweko/kumeneko kuli ana/kumeneko kuli ana/ osasamba, amamina,amanthongo/ kapilire kunka iweko.'

Two shabbily dressed kids who saw us from a mango tree removed me from the jungle of thoughts. They were there like guards to watch over enemies for their eyes were glued to the path. Like cats, they climbed down to welcome us.

"Aunt! Aunt!" They ran towards us. I was surprised that Dora did not tell me the gospel truth about her place.

"Aunt, welcome." The girl said in a local language that I did not speak. After exchanging a few words, immediately, the two children disappeared. I got relaxed when a strange woman came and introduced herself as Dora's mother.

"You are welcome, daughter and son. Feel free."

I asked for a cup of water. Dora went behind the house and after thirty minutes returned with a cup of thobwa. "She says water will not do you good. Take this." (Dora, please know your man. This is your man, not your mother's man. I need water. I spoke to myself). She got a clue that I disliked that decision. She went back and came with what I had asked for. After a while, I gulped down the thobwa. As if by design the mother popped in and sat a few metres away. In fact, she had a lot of sugar-coated stories about her daughter. "She has been refusing men. I don't know what has happened this time. Dude, you are lucky." Namgabi giggled and disappeared to the kitchen.

We spent two nights, nights of misery in which we provided a delicious meal to mosquitoes. I learnt the mother sought warmth in empty maize sacks that were artistically sewn so it could cover a wide radius for the benefit of the children. We were offered one. They slept outside while we were allowed to sleep in the hut. As visitors, they had to ensure our safety not theirs. Throughout the night, I panicked. I could not believe it was happening in a country where some corrupt politicians were misallocating and spending public money to enrich themselves while villagers languished in dire poverty. Why not bring the money to the villagers? Wouldn't that help alleviate some of their life challenges?

Surely, the words sleep and dream did not exist in this region as compared to the comfort I used to enjoy in the city. The place was dark, dreadfully dark at night. Owls and hyenas were terrorizing my peace though I was assured this was nothing to fear. I wish my fiancée had alerted me. Then we could have prepared well to avoid these nasty experiences; we would have been comfortable. But Dora never hinted about this. She was quiet. She did not mention the real life in this village. At least candles, bottled water, duvet, mosquito nets or doom, and a mattress would have solved the puzzle. Whether it was a strategy for me to experience poverty in this way or not, I happened to promise lots of things as soon as possible, that I could provide in less than a week upon reaching the city. I also thought about erecting a better hut than the one I saw.

When we were about to leave around five in the morning of the third day, Dora looked at her mother and hesitantly said.

"She says you will need something. Take these." A packet of flour made from leaves and roots of wild trees.

"You will need nthubulo and gondolosi, my son." Apongozi (Mother-In-law) said. As a professional medical doctor, I had always thought of ways and means of dealing away with myths that some raw roots and rotten leaves had the power of improving fertility. Even traditional medicines did not exist fully in my world. Nevertheless, I quickly resolved how I would sort out these roots of fertility.

"Thanks mum." I said reluctantly. The two kids disturbed my thoughts again.

"Aunt, bye. Uncle, bye." Standing at the door, they whispered in unison.

"Escort them half way. You fool!" Namgabi shouted.

Both Dora and I turned to wave at the mother as we followed a path that went to Miseufolo where we would take kabaza and connect to the main road. That was a shortcut to Mangunda I was told.

Love at first sight

Out of the blues, a figure of a short brown-haired girl in a black skirt and white blouse enters my mind. In a Coca-Cola shape the girl is pushing a wheeled bag commonly known as "an expand" into Wenela bus depot. Pushing her luggage in a hurry, she seems to be late. My heart skips a beat. Through the emergency window of an express bus that is heading north, my eyes follow her as her bottom vibrates shockingly. The bottom together with the owner trots towards the tickets office window. Oh, my...! Since when did angels start trotting visibly on earth? As soon as she faces the door of the bus I am in, I quickly stand up. Angel, 'please sit next to me'. There is a warm seat here. My lips move. She does not hear me. Next her forehead peeps in the bus. 'Come, come baby. Sit next to me'. My lips move again. Thank heavens. She comes straight to where I am. Hallelujah...!

In a twinkle of an eye, I jump and create a space for her. I help her put the bag in its rightful place and at once engage her in a conversation.

"Excuse me, may I know you" I extend my hand towards hers.

She looks at me. She does and says nothing.

"Excuse me, do you speak my language?"

"I am Dora." She says as she welcomes my hand.

"How far do you go?"

"Muhasuwa and you...?"

"Chimulumunde."

In no time, Wenela is out of sight. Afraid of other eagles to catch my fish, I express my wholesale willingness to love her, to protect her and to assure her that all is well in case she had engaged other men who were promiscuous. That is not without an influencing factor, tots of brandy. I am courageous.

"My name is Denis...... Yes Denis."

"Denis, when did you start thinking about me?"

"Just now; love at first sight you know."

"I am afraid. It's too..." She fails to complete the statement as I force her to accept my proposal.

"I don't see any problem. Love birds meet anywhere".

"At a funeral or in a bank...What's the problem meeting in a bus?" She is quiet. Fast as I am, I try to get hold of her hand and pull her close to me. She stares away.

"Denis, do not be crazy."

"Dora, tell me what makes you think I am unsuitable. It appears your heart is laden with uncertainties." I pull her again, but she shrugs her shoulders.

"You are drunk."

"You can also drink and behave equally. I have got plenty here."

"I don't drink and I do not like people who drink." I look at her in the face.

"Believe in change. Everything is possible." She laughs.

The bus inspector arrives to check our tickets. Mine is in the trousers pockets. I show him and he cancels it with green ink. Dora is panicking. She can't trace her ticket. It is neither in her purse nor in her bra. After a long search she remembers that she forgot to collect it from the ticket office. She explains that she came in as the bus was about to leave so she just gave money to the person on the window and rushed in. I remember seeing her through the ticket office window but she is never understood. For life to continue I reached for my pocket and settled the matter. When the inspector passes, I resume the conversation.

"I am suitable, Dora. Try me."

"But you are not responsible."

Suddenly the bus comes to a halt. Muhasuwa Trading Centre waves entertainingly at us. I wave at Dora. She waves back. Before I start forgetting about her, she returns and slaps me hard. I do not believe it.

A Harmless promise to the poor

After an hour of walking to the main road, we sought shelter near a church to rest. I was bidding goodbye to the two children while Dora was quiet. I was promising the two children that they would learn in the city if everything was sorted out according to plan. In fact, they were miserable children whom I thought I would rescue. I learnt this from experience. I grew up in a house where neither the man nor the woman was related to my mother. They also rescued me because my parents could not support me. To tell the truth, I would not be where I was. To hit the nail on the head, they supported me till I left College of Medicine. They encouraged me not to pay back but support my mother. Unfortunately, my mother died as soon as I left the college. I had nobody to trust as my relative since I never saw one in my life except my mother. Therefore, assisting these two orphans would be a good means of paying back. After all, their mother never wished to leave them as young as 4 and 5 respectively. They also did not commit any sin for them to be staying with an old woman miserably.

During my stay there at my mother-in-law's village, I asked where the nearest primary school was located but neither Dora nor her mother were knowledgeable enough to say exactly where the school was. I was told the hospital was in Mangunda; that was almost seven kilometers away. They had no access to clean water for the water that I was drinking smelt of dung. I tried to desist from drinking such unsafe water. But I was very thirsty so I still had to drink it. Of course, I followed instructions that the best way was to have them boiled. In the city, I could not taste it. I reckoned that these two children were indeed at high risk.

"Don't worry I will take care of you. I will send you to Mathambi. It's a nice Private School, have you ever heard about it?" The two children shrugged their shoulders. An indication that they were not even interested in going to school. This reminded me about my early primary school days. I did not like going to school so I was cheating my mum. Taking advantage of the distance, I would get set as if I was indeed going to school when in fact my friends and I would proceed to Gerena Estate; not to peace work as was common then, but just to play. I liked this place because towards lunch hour, we were included and got a share of mgaiwa and nyemba with the workers. We greatly appreciated that we were not asked any questions as to whether we worked at the estate or not. So, when it was revealed that I never registered in standard one, I was being followed closely. Through their eyes I saw a clue that school was something they had given up. I comforted and encouraged them before they left. Believe it or not, a few minutes later, the girl tip-toed behind my back, and struck me with a sharp object. The boy laughed sarcastically. I looked at Dora. She was as usual. Quiet.

While we were still at the shelter, suddenly we saw a police van cruising to a sudden stop. Four police officers escorted by the chief stormed Namgabi's house. Word had been sent to Mangunda police that a lady who alighted at Mafisi one kilometer before Mangunda with a bald-headed short stout man whom they suspected was a foreigner from the neighboring country were hiding at the hut. The report indicated that the lady was the type of those that were being victimized. She did not belong to the village. It was also said that the lady was refusing to leave the spot but the man had pushed her to the forest just to add salt to the injury.

This was thirty minutes after Dora and I had left. The police were following instructions from above that once they find a foreigner travelling in a car or walking with any person living with albinism in an unprotected place, they must shoot to kill.

"Woman, tell us where have they gone?" One police officer pointed a gun at Namgabi.

"This way, Miseufolo" Shivering, Namgabi said.

"Who are they?" Using his gun like a rod, the officer asked while pointing at her.

"I know the woman. She is a prostitute in the city. The man is one of her customers."

"Who is she to you?"

"I am just a caretaker. I am employed to take care of her children. She told me to come here so we can cheat the man better."

The chief heard at once that the children whom the woman known as Namgabi claimed were her grandchildren at the time she was looking for a place to permanently stay were in fact not her real grandchildren. Namgabi had just relocated to this village a week before from where she claimed she was being ill-treated and the chief had been kind to allocate her that piece of land near the hill. Out of the blues, the chief sneezed. Wrinkles deformed his face. He walked round the hut before he pointed his finger at her. "You, liar! Witch!"

Namgabi looked down and spoke. "I am not at fault. I needed money. I was enticed to stop begging in the city and look for a place where I would stay with her children. She pays me from her trade."

"Fast, guys! Catch the greedy woman at the station. She has a case to answer. The officer in-charge of the police team instructed. He further instructed two police officers to run after the foreigner before he killed the woman.

Like famished lions, the two officers quickly run in the direction of their enemy. They nibbled at the distance not only to keep time but to make sure that they got hold of their suspect.

The Bitter Wedding Pill

News about my wedding does not boil down well in my colleague's pot of thoughts. Tamara walks into my office without a knock.

"Denis."

"What?"

"When will you stop picking up street girls for a wife?"

"You do not know? Educated ladies like you are difficult to handle."

"So, it means what I hear is true?"

"What have you heard?"

"About your wedding with that girl, tell me, walimbadi mtima, are you serious if you want to marry her?"

"Umadziwa... nsikidzi ya chikondi ikaluma. (You know when one is submerged in love)" I tell her just to understand when a man loves a woman."

"What was wrong with Martha?"

"Two issues. One, she was not impressive. Two, she was too talkative. It was as if I would add another home theater or another Zodiak in my house."

"So, you feel this town monger is impressive?"

"Yes, I am convinced she is"

"Denis, you will regret it."

"For heaven's sake I swear never to regret."

The wedding ceremony is colourful. Woyerandife church is packed. "Now I declare the D-square, Denis and Dora, man and wife. The moment welcomes cameras, ululations and beating of drums that nearly shake the foundation of the church. At the hall, my mother, apongozi and several friends dish out K1000 notes. I joined her in happiness. Surprisingly, Dora is quiet. I don't care. I mind our wedding business.

I felt the reception delayed us. We had already planned how to spend our honeymoon in style, at a quiet place where if anything only birds or frog wattles would enjoy our company. Till 5 Pm on the dot, we were finally freed. The car that takes us to the honeymoon speeds incredibly fast. I am excited about everything, especially when the car stereo plays a hymn,'yehova mbusa wanga.' Truly, the lord is my shepherd. Upon arrival, Dora's lips creep over mine. She sighs. My girl sighs. I too sigh. Both of us smile at each other. She looks cute. A man and his wife must enjoy it now. I am satisfied I made the right choice. 'How time flies! It is said life is a mountain of mystery. Some people born with a silver spoon in their mouths die poor while others born in the tobacco fields die in executive homes. Something tells me. Denis, you must enjoy it. You have passed through thickets of thorns. Forget about the past. Life is a jigsaw puzzle. What you expect to happen in a day does not exactly happen in your line of thinking. You expect rain, there comes no rain, it is said, but today everything is trailing in its intended path. My new life has begun!

Soon I break into another inward self-conversation.... Life is an avocado pear in a tree. It looks good on one side while the other side is rotten. Dear mum and dad. Glad you made a decision to have me exist. I started nibbling at the rotten side of the cake of life. Take this message to the world. Tell the world that Denis is enjoying it. He is no longer the poor fellow you used to see. Tell the world that now the professional medical doctor is feeling good with Dora. I look at Dora. She is quiet. Before I begin to snore, Dora says; "To show that you love me, give me all the money that has been donated to us or else you will see." I point at the small bag near the drawer. She collects the bag and locks it in her handbag. For three days of our honeymoon, the financial situation. I want to tell her that despite that I am not poor but the wedding collection belongs to both of us. But I hold my breath. What a bitter pill to swallow!

Now you are leaving Mangunda…

"Your mother is very creative." I decided to break the silence when I heard the sounds of moving cars near Mangunda. "What do you think?" I further sought her opinion.

"She was drunk. She had taken tots of Ambuye mtengeni (strong liquor), didn't you observe?"

"No, but I deduced this morning when she was giving us the gondolosi. The woman is a joker." I laughed. Dora was quiet.

I was glad when I reached the main road especially when I saw an ambulance that was heading to the city. I would say I was fortunate because what I thought was just a passenger actually turned out to be a colleague. No sooner had I waved it to stop, than two police officers emerged from the direction we came from. They stopped before us as if they had a mission specifically for us.

"Let's go, Denis." My colleague instructed the driver to start off. The driver obliged.

"These drunkards will delay us." He went on. Dora was quiet. We exchanged a few words with my colleague because while I was the most famous college drunkard, he was the most known college prophet.

We arrived back to town safely.

The Mysterious escape

Today is Sunday. Dora is in the kitchen. I see a tall, light in complexion and not very handsome man pushing the gate in order to let his bicycle in. He has ridges in his hair, giving a hint of wavy hair when it is long. He dons gumboots, a pair of khaki shorts and an oversized shirt. I watch him as his bicycle peeps, shoves forward and perches against the wall. I sit still but patiently peruse the Sunday paper with one eye while the other is on his intentions in my yard. In the shade where I sit, I am carrying a tall glass of old rare brandy mixed with coke. There is a plastic chair reserved for Dora and a coffee table. On the coffee table, a half empty bottle of coca cola leans against a three-quarter full of brandy. On a quiet afternoon like this, I choose to cool off at home and more artistically impress my newly wedded wife than cheer friends whom I had entertained over the years. Confidently, the strange man strolls into the shade and majestically sits on the empty chair without my invitation.

"So, you drink like a boss?" He opens his mouth as he pours some brandy into the Coca-Cola bottle to make it full to the brim till some spills out. I speak nothing, watching him with my right hand holding my chin, I look suggestively at him. Until he pulls two sips, I am not at ease but remain quiet.

"Are you a friend or enemy?" I now break the silence.

"A friend? Haaah!" He pulls another long sip and immediately softens his lips with his tongue. Then he breaks into laughter. Can this be a mad person? Like a security guard, I give him another evocative look with an aim to scare him. But I only realize he is too provocative. Imagine, he moves and sits closer to me. I watch him only to see him taking more moves. Now he takes my glass and quickly gallops all the contents. My eyes turn red. My forehead is full of wrinkles. But all this is met by his lousy smile. I look him straight in the eye. Maybe he will get scared. Alas! He faces away from me, laughing and clapping his dirty hands.

"Have we ever met before?" I want to know.

"Hahahaha! Is that a question for me?" he continues, laughing more loudly than earlier on?"

Before I explain, Dora saunters towards us. I get some courage. At least if he tries to behave more wildly before the two of us then I will share a punch to see day stars before he gets driven out of our compound gate. I will show him all the acrobatics that I was taught by a Chinese person who happened to be a college mate. My heart palpitates faster than usual. I am about to lose my tempers. I hate this nonsense. As caress as he has been. Just imagined how he walks into our premises majestically without any invitation. He also consumed all the food on my table. Without paying much attention to the stranger, Dora serves me with a plate of fried chicken pieces. As soon as their eyes met, Dora hugs the visitor in a long time-no-see fashion. While lifting Dora up, the stranger dances around. Damn it!

"See, how beautiful you are."

"Who told you I was staying here?"

"There is no secret under the sun."

"But tell me when did you step on the Malawian soil from the land of gold?"

"Last week."

I rub my eyes in disapproval. Is it real or am I dreaming? I open my eyes wide to verify whether it is happening live or not. It is reality. Soon I observe that Dora has planted a kiss on the stranger. Please God, save me from evil. What the hell is going on? I gulp down my drink in time to see that the distance between the two lips has widened but nobody seems to be rooted to the spot. But even Dora shows no remorse. They whisper while holding each other. Both are entangled in their love world. Why over all of a sudden, I am now the stranger in my own home? My world is crumbling. Enough is enough. My temper reaches boiling point. I lose control. No more patience Dora! Doora! Doooooooora!

She ignores me. She just looks at me but doesn't answer back. I see her holding hands firmly with the stranger; they go inside our matrimonial home. I now have lost control. My heart misses' beats, in shock I get a sharp object I follow them into the house. There is some noise in the bedroom. Through the back door, I rush into the room. Nobody but a small note in a standard five drop-out pupil handwriting waves on the bed, my bed. "Denis, I married you because you wanted but the truth is what you have just witnessed. He is the man I love." Next the front door bangs. I remove the slippers and put on a flat shoe ready for a race. Upon reaching the front door, I hear the screeching of the gate. I try to open it but both the he-fool and the she-fool have locked it. I stomp to the backdoor. Quickly, I reach the gate. When I get out of the gate, what I see paralyses my limbs. While Dora is seated on the carrier, stylishly, the man rides his bicycle at the Cheetahs speed towards the factories in the industrial area.

***

I woke up from this nightmare at the time when Dora had planted a kiss on me. Her lips were dancing on my nose as if she was licking it.

"Your lips have been moving for two hours now without anything coming out, are you sick?" She said when she saw that I had opened my eyes. I immediately wanted to ask what she was doing at that time for her to notice that my lips had been in motion. I simply avoided her.

"No." I said.

"What time shall we start off to visit Namgabi at Mangunda?"

"Let me think about it."

Mmap Fiction and Drama Series

If you have enjoyed *Stranger In Her Own Skin* consider these other fine books in **Mmap Fiction and Drama Series** from *Mwanaka Media and Publishing:*

The Water Cycle by Andrew Nyongesa
A Conversation..., A Contact by Tendai Rinos Mwanaka
A Dark Energy by Tendai Rinos Mwanaka
Keys in the River: New and Collected Stories by Tendai Rinos Mwanaka
How The Twins Grew Up/Makurire Akaita Mapatya by Milutin Djurickovic and Tendai Rinos Mwanaka
White Man Walking by John Eppel
The Big Noise and Other Noises by Christopher Kudyahakudadirwe
Tiny Human Protection Agency by Megan Landman
Ashes by Ken Weene and Umar O. Abdul
Notes From A Modern Chimurenga: Collected Struggle Stories by Tendai Rinos Mwanaka
Another Chance by Chinweike Ofodile
Pano Chalo/Frawn of the Great by Stephen Mpashi, translated by Austin Kaluba
Kumafulatsi by Wonder Guchu
The Policeman Also Dies and Other Plays by Solomon A. Awuzie
Fragmented Lives by Imali J Abala
In the Beyond by Talent Madhuku
Zororo Risina Zororo by Oscar Gwiriri
Sword of Vengeance by Olatubosun David
Finding A Way Home by Tendai Mwanaka

Your Epistle by Solomon A Awuzie
The Restless Run and Ruin of the Roaches and Rats by McLayode
The Reign of Terror by Ntando Gerald
Ibala Lyabwina Nama by Austin Kaluba
Daddy, Please Don't Kill Mama by Natisha Parsons
Pilate's Angels by Goodenough Mashego
Blue threads and other stories by Matthew Kunashe Chikono
The Sylvia Plath Effect by Abigail George
The Twins by Shakemore Dirani
I, Robert's Robot and other stories by Marvel Chukwudi Pephel
Conversation With My Mother by Wonder Guchu

Soon to be released

https://facebook.com/MwanakaMediaAndPublishing/

www.ingramcontent.com/pod-product-compliance
Lightning Source LLC
Chambersburg PA
CBHW050350030726
47503CB00008B/2702